REVISIONIST FUTURE

REVISIONIST
FUTURE

LEE BUMBICKA

REVISIONIST FUTURE

CamCat
Books

CamCat Publishing, LLC
Brentwood, Tennessee 37027
camcatpublishing.com

This is a work of fiction. Names, characters, places, and incidents are either products of the author's imagination or are used fictitiously.

©2021 by Lee Bumbicka

All rights reserved. Printed in the United States of America. No part of this book may be used or reproduced in any manner whatsoever without written permission except in the case of brief quotations embodied in critical articles and reviews. For information, address CamCat Publishing, 101 Creekside Crossing, Suite 280, Brentwood, TN 37027.

Hardcover ISBN 9780744302134
Paperback ISBN 9780744301205
Large-Print Paperback ISBN 9780744300680
eBook ISBN 9780744322675
Audiobook ISBN 9780744302141

Library of Congress Control Number: 2021931135

Cover and book design by Maryann Appel

5   3   1   2   4

To my wife Debbie

and my children Katy and Mikey

1

THE NEW ENGLAND SHOP

HE DROVE THROUGH THE NIGHT, CHASING the illusive distant light of inspiration. Instead, he found himself on the highway to mental anguish, played out in the arena of the absurd, culminating in a life-and-death struggle with the man who would become his nemesis.

Michael Schatten gazed through the dark and into the clear night sky. His mind was free of thought, and this was his dilemma. His brain, normally alive, painting imagery with all the colors of the English language, was a blank canvas. This was the worst writer's block he had ever known. It had been weeks now since his publisher had so graciously advanced him the funds to pursue his great American novel. At the time, he had it sketched out completely in his mind, but now the concept didn't make any sense.

This, and recent events, prompted him to take a sabbatical, convinced that he had to escape to free his mind and rebuild his shattered life. The divorce was bad enough, but being laid off, taking away his stability, confidence, emotional and economic base, and the work he loved, was too much to bear. It was as if someone was conspiring to test his sanity.

Feeling the desire to be by the Atlantic Ocean, he'd decided to drive to Providence, Rhode Island. The many small towns and scenic highways, which he'd canvassed on the internet, promised the serenity he craved. Schatten had stayed up late searching the net until he found two properties in the small town of Fletcher, just south of Providence. About ten years ago, he had worked in that area of New England for two weeks and thought it was fascinating. Schatten especially recalled the restaurants serving lobster bisque and clam chowder and the old lighthouses. He'd always wanted to return, and now was his opportunity.

Schatten never planned any vacations. He thought that prearranging every detail ruined the adventure. It was one aspect of his personality that exasperated his ex-wife. His obsession with punctuality also infuriated her, as did his habit of looking at his watch during their conversations when she demanded his attention.

So, this time, he hadn't planned anything either, except to drive all night to get to Providence late in the morning, hoping the drive would be therapeutic and provide some stimulus.

But eleven hours into the fourteen-hour trip, his eyelids became heavy, and his car had drifted over the white double lines on more than one occasion. Reaching over to the passenger seat, his fingers probed for a plastic bag containing snacks and caffeinated drinks. He downed two bottles of cola before his body screamed for rest. It was with great relief that he spotted a sign off exit 112 that offered service stations and lodging. He filled his tank, then mustered enough clarity to navigate the distance from the gas pumps to the hotel.

After checking in, he lumbered to his room on the second floor, disdaining the elevator as an affront to his physical conditioning.

Trudging up the steps, dragging his suitcase, he came to the hallway door, which he propped open with one hand while throwing the suitcase into the hallway with the other. Mercifully, his room was only two doors down. He didn't bother to unpack but just plopped onto the bed and fell asleep immediately.

The next day, Schatten explored the region south of Providence off Highway 95 until he found State Highway 1, which allowed him to drive along the coast at a leisurely pace. Pulling down his visor to shield his eyes from the sun, he inadvertently released a piece of yellow note paper he had wedged there the day before. It held the phone number and address of the realtor's office responsible for a beautiful stretch of small vacation spots on the beach.

He pulled over to the shoulder and retrieved the note from the floor, plugged the address into his phone's GPS feature, and followed the female voice's instructions.

A half hour later, he arrived at the realtor's office and parked his car in front.

Schatten walked through the door of the old storefront that served as the entrance to the offices of Hastings Realty and Rental. Seeing no one, he hit the bell at the desk.

A few moments later, a clean-shaven man in his late fifties wearing a T-shirt, shorts, and sandals with slick black hair graying at the temples came out to greet him.

"Can I help you?" he asked.

"Yes, I'm up from Indianapolis and wanted to see if you had something I could rent for a few months," replied Schatten. "Nothing fancy, preferably secluded but close to the beach. I'm writing, trying to finish my book."

"Writ'n a novel, are ya? That would look good in our brochure for sure. Well, young fella, I've got a property down by the water's edge. I can give you a good deal, but it's rough, and I ain't got time to work on it. It's furnished, but no frills. I'll even leave ya the washer and dryer I was gonna move to another place."

"That sounds great. How much?"

"I'll tell you what, you rent it for three months, and I'll let ya have it for eight hundred dollars cash up front."

"Eight hundred dollars a month?" asked Schatten.

"Naw, total. Things are slow right now, and I need cash. I just can't afford to fix the place, so you're helping me out, big time. If you don't take it, it'll just be collectin' dust."

"Now, this place has an air conditioner, stove, refrigerator, and a TV, right?"

"Course it does, but you have to lug the trash up the hill to the dumpster once a week," replied the proprietor. "They collect it every Wednesday, and no one will come in to clean or change the sheets."

"Sold. Where do I sign?"

In exchange for Schatten's eight one-hundred-dollar bills, the man gave him two keys and a receipt along with directions and a map.

The map showed the picture of a lighthouse in close proximity to his cottage, towering over the cove. Some twenty miles from the office he passed it and several minutes later the GPS on his phone announced that he had arrived. Schatten pulled over onto a gravel road to the left which led to a small square parking lot. Schatten got out of his car, scanned the ocean and the surrounding area to see a plastic green dumpster alongside a red steel mailbox, matching the address he had been given. He locked the car and descended a steep hill.

There, some fifty yards straight ahead, was an old, rundown house which only looked worse the closer he came. It was obvious why the property was such a bargain.

Most of the faded white paint had peeled off the old one-story place. Schatten viewed the entire exterior before inserting the key into the front door lock.

As he entered, he felt sponginess beneath his feet. The high tides and driving rain had breached the small gap between the floor and the underside of the front door. The carpet was a testament to the storm's ferocity. The living room exhibited a black Naugahyde couch with a rectangular glass topped coffee table, flanked by a small oak table with a desk lamp on top and a brass floor lamp.

He entered the kitchen and found that the refrigerator, faucets, and light switches were surprisingly functional. There were dishes and standard fare in the drawers and cupboards and a microwave oven above the electric stove.

Turning away from the window, he walked down the narrow hallway toward the bedroom, bereft of blinds or curtains, just like the others. The bathroom, featuring a shower and bath, was just a few feet head. He followed the hallway to a small, open area and the back door. There, he discovered the washer and dryer hidden in a small room just to the right.

His initial survey of the house completed, Schatten decided to bring in his things. He had to make three trips, struggling to navigate the steep incline before bringing in his laptop, which he gently set on the sturdy, wooden kitchen table.

The move-in behind him, Schatten made a list of everything he would need before he ventured into Bedfer, the closest town, for supplies. It took twenty-five minutes to get to the quaint little village. The red stone store fronts, ornate black lampposts, and slow lifestyle seemed to exude New England charm. He slowly drove through the town, surveying all the small stores and restaurants. When he saw the Farmers Market, he parked and went in to stock up on everything from orange juice to frozen dinners. He even found a shower curtain and towels.

Returning to his house, Schatten realized that it would be challenging to trek up and down the hill where he'd parked to unload the groceries. So he searched until he found a gravel road that snaked along a trail to the right, which he took to his back door. He unloaded the car, struggling to open the front screen door that slammed in his face several times during the process.

It was time to explore the surroundings. He put on an old pair of tennis shoes and a worn pair of khaki shorts. He stepped through the front door and stood on the small concrete porch and surveyed the area. There wasn't much beach at his location, and large rocks were everywhere, breaking up the landscape. He looked to his left to discover a pathway winding in and out some three miles toward the lighthouse. He saw no signs of anyone else and realized the extent of his seclusion. Large rock formations formed a wall around the left side of the beach, creating a cove. It wasn't a place for children.

The temperature was in the low eighties as Schatten began his trek down the beach, feeling the surf on his feet and ankles. Seaweed washed up on shore and drifted back and forth with the tide. He walked out up to his knees and felt the powerful tide push him backward. Looking out to sea, he saw a channel that led to the Atlantic. Schatten's house was in a cove near several formidable islands exhibiting steep, jagged solid rock sides, discouraging any boats from landing. As he continued down the coastline, the wind caressed his face and the constant serenade of seagulls provided background music. He had traveled the meandering pathway about two miles before seeing the lighthouse in full view. It was perched atop a rock wall where it looked majestically down on the sea. Schatten wiped his face occasionally when large waves eluded the rocks to splash him. As he reached the lighthouse, he found no easy pathway up the hill; he'd have to scale the rocks.

Schatten had always been fascinated with these icons after reading Jules Verne's *The Lighthouse at the End of the World* about pirates attacking a lighthouse around Cape Horn. He had also seen *The Beast from 20,000 Fathoms*, a 1950s classic where a giant prehistoric monster destroys a lighthouse on the east coast. Smiling at the memory, he began climbing to the base of the house attached to the cone-shaped structure. Once atop the rocks, he stared at the one hundred-foot-high construction. The brick house was painted flat red, as was the tower with the addition of a spiraling, broad white stripe, which encircled it from the base to the top where the huge searchlight was enclosed, surrounded by a railing. He knocked on the door, but no one answered. After an hour spent looking at the edifice from all angles, he began the slow descent to the beach and made his way back to his house.

Once there, Schatten ate his lunch and pulled up the files of his book on his computer. Wading through the forty or so pages he had written so far, he realized the spark still wasn't there. It was as though he was reading someone else's words.

"John Taylor was on the second week of a murder investigation when he made a gruesome discovery . . ."

Uninspired, he decided to search the net for some information on the FBI, the organization that employed his character. He attempted to engage his Wi-Fi when the error message appeared. No network. He had forgotten to ask the realtor about the Wi-Fi.

"What did you expect, a five-star hotel?" he muttered angrily.

He felt like an idiot. His overly trusting nature had often cost him a hefty price, and it was another trait that drove his ex-wife insane. Now he would have to find a coffee shop or go to the library to access the internet. But he could write unencumbered without a network, he'd just have to keep a list of everything he needed to research when he went back to town.

After staring at his laptop for a while, he grabbed the pillows from the bedroom and placed them on the couch, planning to lay down for just a couple minutes. The next thing he knew, it was 5:03 a.m.

He decided to walk on the beach again, hoping to resurrect his lost concept. Barely making an impression in the firm sand during his leisurely stroll in the early morning mist, he skipped rocks out to sea and shivered as the surf hit his ankles. He ventured to the lighthouse once more; he saw it as a symbol of strength, from which he could draw, not just a beacon warning ships and their crews not to venture too close to the shallows.

There was something to be said for the simplicity of its design and how it hadn't changed from the one at Alexandria thousands of years ago, one of the Seven Wonders of the Ancient World. So he began a regiment of walking to the lighthouse in the mornings, hoping this ritual would purge his mind of everything but the story.

But thoughts about his divorce and his last conversation with his boss telling him that he was being terminated kept eroding his creativity. It was during this time that twinges of inspiration would assert themselves, only to dissolve once he sat in front of his laptop. An obscure seafaring character would arise, only to fade into oblivion just minutes later. So on the third day, still uninspired, he decided to go into town and have breakfast at one of several intriguing little restaurants he'd seen.

He selected Mark's Diner, a 1950s style place featuring a 1957 Chevrolet, curb or walk-in service, and an old-fashioned soda fountain. The concrete building was painted light blue with speakers mounted on poles with menus in ten locations where one could place an order without getting out of their car. But Schatten elected to walk inside and sat in one of the booths, Elvis blaring. The service was fast, and he consumed his pancakes in short order. He decided to walk through town before going back to yet another uninspired writing session and was pleasantly surprised to discover a small antique shop on the far side of town. Pressing his face against the window, with hands cupped to shield his eyes from the glare, he saw a collection of everything from cuckoo clocks, muskets, bullets of all descriptions, helmets, model ships and airplanes, vintage toys, flintlocks to a bronze diver's helmet, and a mind-numbing potpourri of souvenirs and historic memorabilia. Intrigued, he pressed the latch and opened the old wooden door, triggering the bell that announced his entry.

"Mornin'," said a voice from the rear of the shop.

"Good morning," Schatten replied.

The shopkeeper, a white-haired, bearded man of small stature dressed in a white shirt and coveralls, approached him. Schatten's first impression was that the individual was the perfect curator for the vintage collection; an old man who'd seen it all with stories to tell about each item in his store.

"You see anythin' that strikes your fancy, don't hesitate to ask."

For a brief moment, Schatten thought that he had met the man before or at least someone who resembled him.

"Thank you, I will."

Schatten canvassed the small shop from corner to corner. There were boxes of Clark Bars, Forever Yours Bars, and other candy he remembered as a kid. Toy airplanes, tin soldiers, frogmen, a plastic submarine, a stuffed alligator, and a metallic chess set were in evidence. His eyes were transfixed upon the diving helmet that was just to the right of the display window. It reminded him of Jules Verne's *Twenty Thousand Leagues Under the Sea*.

"Got that from a sponge diver after his last dive, just before he retired," said the owner, noticing Schatten's interest.

"Uh, how much for this?"

Schatten had always had a secret desire to own one of these.

"Thirteen hundred and seventy-five dollars for that one."

"Ouch."

Refocusing, Schatten began to look over other areas of the store. He went down every aisle, unable to contain a grin that reminded him of his childhood going through his favorite toy shop or an old Army Navy store with his dad. He felt as if he were in a 1940s or '50s exhibition when he came across several rusty handcuffs, a dozen old hand-cranked wall telephones along with a mechanical calculating device and a few American and Japanese bayonets and helmets. Suddenly, between some dummy hand grenades and an IBM desktop computer, he had a glimpse of part of something that caught him off guard. Partially exposed, it was buried in the farthest corner of the store, under cardboard and metal recruiting posters and speed limit signs. He set the signs aside, rearranged the Halloween masks, an old broom, and a pot that look like a witch's cauldron to expose an old typewriter. He could envision it in the hands of Edward R. Morrow during World War II London broadcasts or some other famous correspondent or writer; perhaps even Hemingway.

Inexplicably, his mind exploded with thought. This could be the key to unlock his inspiration.

The storeowner had been continuously jabbering in the background as Schatten navigated the store isles, but the moment he bent over this device, the man fell silent.

"How much do you want for that?" asked Schatten, pointing to the device. "I think I could really write with this."

The old man made his way from behind the counter and approached him. "How much you willin' to pay?"

"Oh, I don't know, twenty bucks?"

"I mean, how much are you really willin' to pay for what you want?" the old man inquired.

Schatten felt uneasy under the man's stare. The cryptic question didn't help matters, and he felt the urge to leave. "Maybe I better go. I've got work to do."

"Okay, if that's what you want. But this could be just what you came here for . . . to finish the book."

Schatten stopped dead in his tracks. "How do you know I'm working on a book?"

"Well, are ya or ain't ya?" continued the shopkeeper in his thick New England brogue.

"Yeah, I am, but how did—"

"How did I know?" interrupted the proprietor. "Who else would be lookin' for a typewriter?"

"Maybe I'm a collector."

"No, you're a writer, alright," said the man. "We both know why you're lookin' at this."

"Why don't you tell me."

"You can't think, and you can't write, and that's why you came here. And this'll do it for ya, I guarantee it. But like I said, what price are ya willin' to pay?"

"Like *I* said, twenty bucks," Schatten challenged.

"Okay, sport, twenty dollars it is. Cash only."

Schatten fumbled, trying to remove his wallet from his jeans. He wrestled it out, and his fingers grasped the first twenty-dollar bill he saw, which he immediately presented to the owner.

"I don't give receipts," said the man.

"Well, what if it doesn't work?" said Schatten.

The old man smirked. "Oh, it'll work . . . all too well, young man."

He lifted the unit and handed it to a befuddled Schatten. "Got any questions, ya know where to find me. Don't come in on Thursdays, though, that's when we go fishin'." The man escorted Schatten to the door. "Thanks for comin'. We've waited a long time for ya. Have a nice day, and enjoy our piece of the country."

"You've waited for me? What do you—?" But before he could finish his sentence, the old man had closed the door behind him and locked it. Schatten watched him put the CLOSED sign in the window.

"Weird."

Schatten carried his antique to his car, reached into his pants, and pulled out the car keys and unlocked his trunk. He gently wrapped his new acquisition in a blanket for protection and placed it into the trunk. As he proceeded to the cottage, he was more hopeful than ever for a breakthrough. Some twenty-five minutes later, he unlocked the door to the beach house and immediately placed his purchase on the couch. Then he set out to rearrange his furniture to create a good spot for writing. After setting the lamp on the floor, Schatten slid the small table over to the window just left of the couch to overlook the beach. He placed the typewriter on top and pulled over a chair from the kitchen. The antique machine was covered in dust, and so he retrieved a dishrag and cleaned away every trace of dirt, sneezing several times during the process. At least now he could read the make and model.

Schatten opened the window and positioned himself in the padded chair in front of his now spotless acquisition. His fingers felt the contours of every key as he slowly began to work each and every one. He picked up a block of printer paper that he also used for his notes and fed a sheet into the device.

He wondered how long it had been since he had done that. He glanced toward his laptop on the kitchen table as if it could see what he was doing and couldn't help but quip, "This isn't permanent, you're still my buddy."

As though waiting to be engulfed by some enormous tidal wave of brilliance, he positioned his hands just above the keys and remained motionless.

"It ain't that easy," he mumbled to himself, suddenly realizing that the machine would not write by itself.

Sitting transfixed, staring at the ocean, listening to the seagulls vying for food and the rhythmic pulsing of the waves, he slowly began to relax. Clearing his mind, and resting his fingers on the keys, he began to play with words, like an artist dabbing paint on a canvass. Beginning by simply putting the keys through their paces and typing each letter, he followed by typing who, what, and where? Schatten felt a twinge as he typed Preson, Parsons, Jack Preston and then John Preston and finally John Prescott.

"John Prescott was a bewildered man," he continued, "who loved the sea, loved the sea as Melville loved her, as did his forefathers."

Before he knew what was happening, his mind created a character as a mental form began to show itself, chiseled by the writer's freed creativity. The dead calm that had pervaded his mind for so many weeks had given way to the steadily blowing wind of inspiration, filling the sails of his imagination. Ideas were pouring out of him now with such rapidity that he could barely make his fingers touch the keys fast enough to capture the thoughts as they leaped from his mind.

The character that suddenly popped into his head was so vivid that in a few hours, it felt as though he had always known the man. He was a craftsman, a renaissance man, who came to New England in search of an identity. He was drawn to the sea as was Ishmael in *Moby Dick*, but in this contemporary version of the tale, left Wall Street and all its stagnate trappings and complications to find adventure and a sense of purpose in the Atlantic's mystical power and vastness. Among other things, the character, John Prescott, was rebuilding a boat. It had been blown out to sea from reaches unknown, traveling hundreds of miles before running aground on the beach in his front yard.

The nameless small craft gave no indications of the previous owner and had a gaping hole in its side. Dragging it ashore and beginning its renovation, he found a hundred-dollar bill nailed to the inside of one of the planks while removing some of the rotted wood. The hull was about twenty feet in length, and it stood some six feet wide. It featured a sail at the bow of the vessel and space enough for two people to sleep below deck or to get out of the weather. The dark green paint had faded and flaked, and the weather and the sea had taken their toll.

Schatten chronicled the man's daily routine and created a beautiful woman who became his Eve. They met as Prescott sat having breakfast in a little downtown diner, while celebrating his good fortune.

"Hi, my name is Stephany Adams. I hate eating alone," she said to Prescott. "Is anyone sitting here?"

"Please," he responded as he rose and pulled out the other chair. "You timed your arrival perfectly; I needed someone to help me celebrate."

"Celebrate what?" she asked flashing her incredible smile.

"This," he said smiling, reaching into the pocket of his jeans and unfurling a tattered one-hundred-dollar bill. "I found this tacked to Matilda."

"Who is Matilda? Should I be jealous?" she smirked. She prided herself on her ability to analyze people based on first impressions, and she liked what she saw in Prescott.

Prescott laughed. "She's my boat, my restoration project."

Schatten went on to write that the boat was a nautical version of the genie in the bottle, as it would magically take Prescott and Adams on an epic adventure, restoring his faith in mankind and reassessing his self-worth and his values like trusting, helping others, loyalty, and simply doing what's right.

His days on Wall Street had eroded his morality and replaced it with a dog-eat-dog mentality. Prescott was beginning to view everyone as a competitor with no time for friends or meaningful relationships.

Schatten wrote steadily for hours before suddenly feeling fatigue in his neck. Pleased with himself, he stretched and rose from his chair. Deciding to walk on the beach, Schatten hoped to fill in some chapters in his mind before putting any more on paper.

Suddenly realizing that he was producing hard copy and couldn't edit with electronic ease, he became slightly disenchanted, but he tried to tell himself that it would be a simple matter to scan everything or hire an assistant to retype it to a file on his laptop. He wondered how previous generations conducted business using these old machines back in the day and gained a better appreciation for those who did.

He slipped off his shoes and proceeded down the beach. Schatten glanced at his watch and noted that four hours had passed since he'd begun writing. As he breathed in the salt air and felt the sensation of the sand under his feet, he looked at the vastness of the Atlantic Ocean and listened to the waves continue to provide their metrical mantra. But when he walked out too far and a large wave suddenly appeared to knock him off his feet, Schatten felt reminded of its power. He was enjoying his ocean experience, nonetheless.

As he considered turning back after a walk further along the beach, Schatten came upon a small, nondescript, ordinary house close to the water. Just past the house was a small boat, resting on the sand. He didn't remember seeing any houses on his drive when he had surveyed the landscape a few days earlier.

As he approached the boat, he couldn't control the over-whelming sense of déjà vu. There was something familiar about the skiff, but he couldn't quite place where he had seen it before.

It was roughly twenty feet in length and about six feet across. It had a single sail once attached to the bow, now lying beside the craft. It had a small area below deck large enough to hide from the weather. But the deck area had eroded to the point that much of it would require replacement as would the rotting hull. It was painted green, but much of it was flaking with a gaping hole in its hull around the bow.

His mind was fighting what his eyes were telling him; what a bizarre coincidence. Theorizing that it must belong to the owner of the house, he decided he would meet the occupants. Schatten walked up to the door and knocked, but there was no response. He peered through the front window but saw nothing to indicate that it was occupied. He looked at his watch—it was five o'clock. Time to turn back.

Arriving home, he immediately sat down at the typewriter, overcome by a sudden urge to get his thoughts on paper. His mind was alive now, and he wrote uninterrupted for three more hours. Schatten added a garage to his character's house and detailed the interior of the workshop and the tools that Prescott had amassed to overhaul his boat. He described the house and, more specifically, the exterior. It was one bedroom with two windows on the front facing the ocean and one on each of the sides. It had faded yellow siding and pale green shutters on the front two windows. The left shutter was in need of repair and hung down. The front and back doors were also painted pale green.

When he was done, he folded his arms on the table and rested his head atop them as a sudden rush of fatigue consumed him.

The next thing he knew, it was morning as he stretched and shook his head.

"So much for writer's block," he said, grinning.

He felt a cramp in his neck and right shoulder from sleeping in such a weird position, and so he rotated his arms and moved his head in all directions.

The sunrise on the ocean was too much to resist. He stretched and hurried out the door onto the beach. Suddenly remembering the boat, he walked down the beach to the location where he had found it hours before. His senses were now beginning to awaken as he shivered from the surf enveloping his feet and the wind's caress. He turned to see his footprints in the sand being brushed away by the tide as sandpipers and hermit crabs scurried about, and the seagulls relentlessly screeched as they effortlessly rode the wind in search of their next meal. No ominous clouds were discernable as his eyes absorbed the glorious sunrise with red and purple hues rebounding off the huge billowy, white formations.

He kept up a steady pace to see if his powers of recollection were reliable or if he had merely conjured the craft in his sleep. As he approached the site, his heart quickened as he saw that it was still there. But now there was something new and perplexing. The day before, the house was a simple, unadorned white and totally unremarkable. In fact, had anyone given him a quiz to describe the features of the house, he would have been hard pressed to answer one question correctly.

But as he looked at the house from the front it was as though someone had substituted the other house with his creation. It was pale yellow with pale green shutters on the front windows. There was now a garage, and what was most disturbing, the appearance of the left shutter hanging down in disrepair.

He walked over to the boat, which was positioned just a few feet from his new neighbor's dwelling. Schatten began to scrutinize the skiff. It was a nice boat, faded green with white trim and in reasonable condition, save for the breech in its hull, rotting deck, and flaking paint—a remarkable coincidence to be sure.

It was too early to knock on the door. There was no car to indicate if anyone even occupied the house, so any questions as to the origin of the craft would have to wait. For a few moments, he contemplated searching for the money under the hull, but finding it would have pushed his paranoia too far. He had always prided himself on logical thinking, and so he tried to dismiss this whole sequence as a disconcerting quirk and an ironic happenstance that would soon be forgotten.

He headed back to his cottage, where he decided to take a shower before going into town. But before he turned on the water, he opted to sit down at the typewriter once more. He realized that his character had no means of transportation, and so he decided to give him a car.

"How about a BMW?" he mused. "Yeah, a red convertible . . . why not?"

Then he continued to fill in more details regarding his character, his physical description

—six foot two, 195-pound frame—his predilection for seafood, and his view of humanity. Schatten then fleshed out Stephany Adams' features and biography.

Then he stopped and reviewed what he had written the night before. Chills raced up his spine. He couldn't be in denial forever; what he had seen on the beach was the craft from his story—it was Matilda, John Prescott's boat resting on the beach at John Prescott's place.

Stunned, he stepped away from the typewriter and stared at it. After a few minutes of that standoff, he shook his head as if to rid himself of these crazy thoughts and decided to take a shower to wash away the events that challenged his sanity. He decided that there was a perfectly reasonable explanation, but he wouldn't waste his time to try to figure it out. He was making great progress on the story; that was all that mattered.

2
THE CAST OF CHARACTERS

Driving down the scenic highway into town, Schatten felt that his first impression was right: The old machine had provided the stimulus he needed to lift him from the depths of literary depression to a new level of confidence in his ability to write. Finishing the book was all that mattered, and the bizarre byproducts were mere distractions. Surveying a portion of the little town in his car, he decided to stop at a small café on the water's edge. He checked his watch and discovered that the restaurant wouldn't open for another hour.

So he drove into areas of the town that he had never frequented, searching for a place that was serving. When he came upon a small vintage diner, he was delighted to see the "Open 24 Hours" sign in the window. Schatten parked across the street, ambled up three wooden steps and onto the blue porch, replete with three rocking chairs and a swing.

"Sit anywhere you like," said the waitress as Schatten entered. He perused the interior and selected a booth close to the window. Schatten was already mentally spent from the previous night and his early morning activities. It was a welcome respite to sit casually in the booth scanning the menu while purging his mind of everything but food. There was a counter with swivel chairs, several tables, and no loud music.

He happened to look up from the list of offerings as a tall, dark-haired man entered and sat down at a table nearby. A few minutes later, a beautiful young woman entered, clad in jeans with a white sweater and brown boots, her long blonde hair in a ponytail. She surveyed the room before proceeding to the table where the young man had positioned himself only moments earlier.

Thinking that anyone would be lucky to have such a stunning girlfriend, Schatten found what looked like an appetizing meal and motioned to the waitress that he was ready to order. As the waitress acknowledged his signal, he could hear the conversation between the handsome couple.

"Hi, my name is Stephany, Stephany Adams. I hate eating alone. Would you mind if I joined you?" she said. "Is anyone sitting here . . . Mister?"

"Prescott, John Prescott," the man responded shaking her hand. "Please." He rose and pulled out the other chair.

Schatten spit up his mouthful of orange juice before coughing excessively. Schatten signaled that he was okay as the waitress rushed to his table to assist him.

The two had flawlessly repeated the entire dialogue he had composed the previous afternoon. Schatten tried to rationalize every illogical event that he had encountered so far, but it became all too apparent that these were *his* characters repeating *his* words. The appearance of the one-hundred-dollar bill which Prescott proudly displayed left no doubt: the old typewriter was magically producing real images.

He tried not to stare and levy attention upon himself, but he had to note every detail of their features, as well as their mannerisms and speech. He could hardly contain himself, for it was as if he were watching his children from a distance—children he had never met or seen. How many authors would give anything to see their characters brought to life; to hear their voice inflections, see their facial expressions, mannerisms, and emotions?

He had a vivid mental picture of these two people, and these performers exhibited every aspect of his imagined profile.

"What brings you here, Stephany?" asked Prescott.

"I'm a fashion designer, starting my own business. How about you?" asked Stephany.

"I'm taking a sabbatical," he responded.

"To do what exactly, and for how long?" she asked.

"I'm running away from Wall Street to find John Prescott and his destiny. Shouldn't take any longer than . . . oh, a couple decades," he laughed, causing her to laugh.

Schatten was beside himself with joy, relishing the experience while being scared out of his wits. He wasn't just generating inanimate objects; he was creating people!

"Where did you move from?" asked Prescott.

"Well, I escaped from New York, like you, and ended up in LA. I felt like I was always under a microscope, being judged for what I was wearing, what I wasn't wearing, and being forced to hang out with the beautiful people. I couldn't stand the hypocrisy and being told what to do twenty-four seven. Now I do what I want with whom I want and wear what I want. Okay, your turn," she said.

"I saw my life like an hourglass, with the sand slipping away. I decided to turn it on its side and stop the flow. I had everything I sought but never had time to enjoy what I had or do what I wanted. I felt like the fox—always one step ahead of the hounds but never pausing to rest or see the world. My clients loved what I did for their bank accounts, but the competition was so fierce that I made few friends. I was meticulous in my research on businesses and the market, but when you're good, everybody thinks that you're scamming and cheating. My research now involves learning how to overhaul boats. So here I am, putting everything on hold, thinking that I might sail to the Panama Canal for starters."

Somehow, Schatten managed to finish his meal while listening to their conversation as discreetly as possible. Sometimes he would mouth the words under his breath as he listened to the dialogue. He couldn't help but stare at them but quickly turned away when he made eye contact. When it seemed that they were getting ready to leave, Schatten scrambled to exit before them and took a position across the street in his car to wait for them to emerge from the diner. He waited for just under an hour, but he didn't care. He observed a red BMW convertible parked out front, top down, identical to the one he had envisioned for the character.

When they finally exited, the couple climbed into Prescott's convertible and drove away. Schatten followed the two as they led him to the beach, where Prescott's boat rested on the sand. He recalled writing that Prescott parked in a small lot close to the path that led down to the man's house. Schatten parked on the shoulder of the highway within thirty yards and endeavored to be as unobtrusive as possible. But was it spying if he created them? He got out of his car and watched Prescott and Adams leave their car and descend down the path leading to the boat. Then Schatten sprinted behind a tree by Prescott's car before following their path, stopping behind every tree and large rock.

Trying to recall their specific conversation at this juncture, Schatten failed to pick up most of what was being said. Occasionally he would hear some loud outburst like Stephany laughing and blurting out, "You're not serious?" as Prescott responded, "You can't make that up!" Schatten took a position behind several boulders and a cluster of trees just above Prescott's house. He watched the two make their way down the gravel pathway to the back of the cottage. Schatten felt like the paparazzi surreptitiously observing the vivid living portrayal of the stars of his writings. They walked to the front of the house as Prescott unlocked the door. The two entered the garage as Schatten recalled the gist of their conversation, and Prescott showed Stephany Adams his arsenal of tools he had acquired to work on his beloved boat. Schatten strained to hear the dialogue, but the building made it impossible. Then the couple emerged, and he showed her his boat. Schatten crept down the path and found another tree behind which to hide.

"So this is Matilda?" asked Stephany.

"One and the same. Isn't she beautiful?" said Prescott, stroking the craft like a pet.

"Gorgeous," replied Stephany, looking at the hulk. "And you're sailing to Panama, in this?" She paused.

"Oh ye of little faith," quipped Prescott, grinning.

Prescott then took her hand, and the two took off their shoes and walked the beach to the right of the craft until they disappeared into a region that Schatten hadn't yet explored.

He ran to a rock wall and caught the last glimpse of the couple. The landscape was open from here and so it was impossible to conceal himself.

He heard Stephany's voice break into laughter and heard her yell, "Oh stop, stop," in unconstrained laughter.

"No, seriously, he drank almost all of it before the dog could finish!"

Schatten recalled this true story of a St. Bernard that loved gin and would lap up drinks left unattended at parties. He could not eavesdrop further without being conspicuous, and so he walked back to his car and drove to his beach house. Once he arrived, Schatten sprinted inside to reread his text. He realized that what he had heard and seen was an exact replication of all he had written. The dialogue took place in the restaurant, the car and ended on the beach.

He sat down and began to write furiously, growing the plot, expanding the dialogue, and creating new characters.

Several days passed as he witnessed his writings brought to life. Any characters that Schatten conjured up were flawlessly reproduced in the world around him. He created a navy veteran, Jacob Allen, who owned a local real estate office and rented Prescott his cabin. He and Prescott would have breakfast together once a week where he would regale Prescott with sea stories and give him pointers about refurbishing the boat. Schatten remembered the waitress patting Prescott on the back and asking if he wanted more coffee. This was significant since he hadn't written any dialogue between his character and the waitress; only between his characters.

He enjoyed seeing other creations like an elderly gas attendant and former merchant marine, Bob Verk, joke with Prescott at the pump on how expensive fuel was in comparison to the Fifties and a cocky car salesman, Jonas Schmidt, attempt to impress Stephany at a car dealership, only to be humbled by her knowledge and wit. The words flowed from his mind, suddenly fertile with concepts, situations, and characters.

Schatten had tapped into a virtual sea of creative ideas. He was certain to finish his novel without the need for further inspiration. The typewriter had done its job.

So, he decided to return to his laptop. What was the point of using this old fossil? It wasn't like he had to see every scene reenacted. In fact, he hadn't seen most of the story, although he did visit the boat every day to check on the progress. But unless he wrote about the labor performed, the craft just sat there, suspended in time.

As the hours passed and the story continued to evolve, Schatten became concerned and ill at ease. He began to question who these newly minted people really were.

Schatten ventured into town for answers. He had written a scene where the couple met in the diner once more, where he could observe them. When they had eaten and left the facility, he approached the counter to pay his bill. Then he asked the manager about the identities of the two individuals that had just exited his establishment. The proprietor responded that he didn't think they were from around there but had seen them on one other occasion.

Then he commented on the curvaceous nature and elegance of the woman, to which Schatten smiled and nodded like a proud father. He asked several other people in the facility the same question and received a similar response. Thus he had a partial answer in his own mind that these individuals may have had no existence or substance other than for a moment . . . or rather, the moments that he had created for them.

But what became of them when he was not around? Did they exist independently of his presence? It was far too improbable to assume that he had run into them by happenstance at exactly the moment he had written for them. Granted, he had composed the sequence in the restaurant at a specified time so he could time his own visit to coincide, but what about the very first encounter?

Revisionist Future

Schatten knew it was time to meet his main characters to investigate his burning question: Had he, through the strange device masquerading as a typewriter, been allowed to create actual living, breathing beings that would continue to survive, even after he put the work aside?

He went back to his cottage and walked down to the area of the beach where the boat and house from his story resided. The craft was under reconstruction, precisely as written. He knocked on the door, but no one answered. As in the book, the boat was supported on a wooden platform, and several pieces of the hull had already been replaced, consistent with his description. Suddenly, his character appeared with tools in hand and started fashioning some replacement parts for various sections of the boat. Schatten had waited long enough and summoned the courage to approach him.

"Nice boat," he said, staring at the man.

Prescott never wavered in his labor and totally ignored him. Suddenly, Stephany emerged from the garage.

"Good morning, I'm Michael Schatten," he said extending his hand. She ignored his overture and began a dialogue with Prescott.

Schatten stepped between the two and passed his hand in front of Prescott's face. No reaction.

It was clear that Schatten was unable to immerse himself into the story and interact with his characters. Shakespeare couldn't become Macbeth, apparently. But did this mean they did not have real substance? Schatten tried touching Stephany's shoulder but felt nothing but air. Were they mere figments of his imagination? Was he hallucinating? Going crazy? Was someone playing a trick on him?

Schatten decided to write no more of Prescott's storyline for several days. Instead, he would start another novel with a different plot and see what it produced. Schatten decided to push the envelope of what he could do with his genie in a keyboard. When he arrived home, he started writing another story. This one concerned whaling ships of the eighteen hundreds. He wrote of the vessel passing by his shore in full sale.

He began to write:

> The year was 1879, and the whaling ship, Arrow, was returning from her two-year voyage at sea, carrying the scars of her adventures. She was now in the waters off the east coast trying to make New Bedford at all speed, hampered by the loss of her main sail, crushed by the gales of the north Atlantic.

Since the shoreline was relatively shallow, he knew that any large vessel would be far out into the channel. As he wrote, he continuously glanced out the window, looking for the signs of masts and sails. An hour later, he interrupted his writing to grab a cold bottle of water from the refrigerator. He went down to the beach to feel the ocean air. Hours passed, and his hope sank. He laid back on the sand and closed his eyes for a few minutes, until he felt the urge to walk. He got up and took a few steps in the sand when suddenly, a few hundred yards out to sea, a huge craft with three masts appeared. Black with white trim, it cut through the water as its sails filled with the wind, save the broken main mast. Shielding his eyes from the sun, he could see the small boats used to track down the whales. There was the figurehead on the bow, which appeared to be an Amazon warrior pulling back on her bow, just as he had written. He saw the lookouts in the crow's nest, high above the deck, looking for reefs and heard them call out their observations to the captain, Horas Branigan, and first mate, Marshal Lowe. Schatten stood in awe as the craft made its way; the sails filled with the sea air and crew members busy carrying out their duties as the ship sailed out of sight and around the peninsula that jutted out a mile up the bay.

"Unbelievable."

He raced back into the house and sat at the keyboard once more, feverishly trying to figure out what else he could invoke. He created a World War II sequence with obscure aircraft such as the P-61 Black Widow and other planes flying overhead. He didn't bother to create any characters, merely the scene of the fighters flying at low level and in formation. The moment he was done, he raced outside, intently searching the skies, waiting for the sound of the radial engines to break through the serene setting, but to no avail. Suddenly, consumed with an unconstrained zeal to generate all manners of things and demonstrate his prowess of creation, he began to spew out short treaties on varying subjects. Obsessed with his new-found power—and in an attempt to convince himself that anything was possible—his fingers busily sculpted a cavalcade of animate and inanimate objects and vignettes that he hoped would soon become reality. He authored Vikings coming ashore, prehistoric beasts roaming the countryside, and a pirate ship anchoring to dispatch a longboat to bury treasure on his doorstep.

But he sensed something was wrong, for he no longer felt the connection with the device. Instead, it was as though his prose were empty and meaningless; devoid of the passion that he had put into Prescott's saga and his whaling yarn. He began to realize that he had an emotional attachment to Prescott, his original creation, and his love for ships had warmed him since he was a boy. He had written with conviction, but the dispassionate drivel he was now composing lacked anything of substance. Could it be that he had not laid enough groundwork and provided inadequate detail?

He was very confused, for every time Schatten thought that he understood the machine, whatever it was, it con-founded his logic.

Compelled to touch base with his creation, he walked down the beach to check in with John Prescott. The sun was hot, and the sky clear as he ventured upon the seemingly endless stretch of sand dotted with large rocks and seaweed. Occasionally, he would throw a rock out to sea and watch the sandpipers and hermit crabs scurry about looking for a meal.

He was enjoying himself, feeling totally relaxed, as he came upon the location of the little house and the boat under repair. Schatten was sure he had come to the right spot, but the house was gone; vanished along with the boat, the car, and Prescott.

He was relieved—sanity had been restored. But then again, did this mean he had been hallucinating in these last few days? No, his experiences had seemed so real. Or did this mean that any life given by the typewriter was short-lived? Yes, that had to be it. Unless the story continued, the cast was put away like marionettes until the next performance.

This presented quite a conundrum. Should he carry on with the old typewriter or not? Should he give life to characters that ultimately would be cast aside—killed off as it were—if he did not keep writing them? Was he ready to take on such power over life and death?

The answer was surprisingly easy. He owed his publisher a novel, and time was slipping through his fingers. Prescott was an interesting character, and the relationship to Stephany had room to grow. Prescott could be the splendid hero of a thriller and Stephany his damsel in distress. Yes, he needed that novel, and he needed it fast. The advance he'd been paid would be gone soon enough, and the little bit of literary credibility he had accrued would be gone with it. And to say nothing of his wife's Schadenfreude if he turned out to be the failure she'd always suspected he was.

He returned to his place, still in deep deliberation. Suddenly, his train of thought was shattered by the roar of engines as a black silhouette appeared in the sky just overhead and streaked by at tree-top level. As it passed, he noticed that it had twin engines, a split tail and the distinctive lone gun turret with four machineguns atop the center fuselage. It was a vintage P-61 World War II night fighter, dubbed the Black Widow, a prize by any collector's standard. He'd never seen one operate before, and it was exhilarating.

That's when a horrible thought crossed his mind . . . As if awakened from a drunken stupor, he realized the potential chaos he had wrought in the guises of Vikings, pirates, and dinosaurs. How could he sleep knowing that someone might wake to a Viking or pirate blade at his throat or as the meal to an Allosaurus? Although *he* might be impervious and insulated from his creations, what if others were not? What if a child had been present or a family? They might have been slaughtered!

What if he wrote of a car chase with Prescott escaping from his enemies and an old woman was crossing the street and was struck? Or another car veered off the road to avoid them and plunged down a gorge? He had already envisioned a scene as Prescott and Stephany sailed Matilda along the east coast where they barely eluded an exploding warehouse where several were killed or maimed. What if the building had people inside or nearby?

Before he could think any further about his potential predicament, he saw the sail of a wooden vessel and the site and sound of many oars hitting the water. The distinctive head of a dragon adorned the front of the ship and it had all the earmarks of a Nordic vessel. Soon the ship came to shore as twelve Viking warriors leaped onto the beach with swords drawn. Schatten ran for his life. He hid behind several large trees and watched from afar as the marauders milled about, not finding anything to pique their interest . . . other than the beach house.

"The typewriter!"

Panic was now the code of the day as all rationality vaporized. He tried to remember what he had written. Surely he hadn't written about them attacking his domicile. If they entered the house and found nothing, they might very well carry off the typewriter as a curiosity . . . or worse, destroy it. What had he done?

The raiders, clothed in skins and brandishing weapons, searched the area briefly before training their attention on the house. The marauders milled about outside while Schatten's heart sank. He couldn't let them take or destroy his prize.

Sprinting to the back door, he raced straight to the typewriter. Before the barbarians systematically searched every room, he grabbed the typewriter from the living room and bolted for the back door. Holding his breath, he prayed that they would quickly discern that there was nothing of value and occupy their attention elsewhere. He entered the hallway to the back door and was just a few feet from freedom.

Seemingly out of nowhere, Schatten was suddenly confronted by a large hulk of a man who smelled like a buffalo. He glared in Schatten's direction but didn't draw his sword. Schatten could not delay; he took the offensive and charged directly at the man like a fullback trying to cross the goal line. As he braced for impact, he passed directly though the man and almost fell on his face, slamming against the screen door frame before sprinting for the safety of the trees.

Thankful that, apparently, he was immune to anything he wrote, he stopped to catch his breath.

Within minutes, the men were gone as they manned their oars once more and presumably headed for a place worth ravaging.

Schatten did a quick mental inventory of everything that had transpired. He was becoming too engrossed in the machine when his obsession should have been to finish his book. He could not keep writing with it or even keep it, for if someone stole it and composed a terrorist plot—blowing up a ship or a plane—there could be hundreds of collateral injuries and deaths. His imagination ran circles around him until he was ready to realize that the best recourse was to return it.

3

A QUEST FOR ANSWERS

SCHATTEN DIDN'T WASTE ANY TIME driving into town. He carefully lifted the typewriter from the trunk of his car and carried it through the doorway of the shop where he'd purchased it just days before. As the bells announced his entry into the mystical little store, he searched for the owner. Seemingly materializing out of nowhere, the little man appeared behind him.

"Brought the thing back, have ya, young fella?"

"Uh, yeah I have," said Schatten. He had so many questions, but now that he was here, he wasn't sure where to begin.

"Kind of a unique item, ain't it?"

"Yeah, you could say that."

"Helped you get goin' again, though, didn't it?"

"Oh, it did that," Schatten replied. "Look, can I just get my money back on this?"

"Is that all you want, your money? Nothin' else? I figured a smart young man such as yourself would have a long list of questions by now. But maybe I figured you wrong."

"What do you mean by that?"

"I mean, I thought you were the sort that would be on a quest for answers," said the proprietor.

"Well, yeah I am, sort of," said Schatten.

"You didn't get wrapped up in what ya saw, did ya?"

"Wrapped up . . . what do you mean?"

"You didn't use it for your own gain. That shows character."

"You mean I wasn't stupid enough to monkey around with the occult or whatever this thing is? No, you're right." Schatten started rubbing the back of his neck. The shop owner seemed to be toying with him, enjoying his discomfort.

The man let out a hearty laugh. "Oh my, that's a goodin'!"

"What?"

"Occult," said the man, still chuckling.

"Do you mind explaining what you mean?" Schatten demanded, his eyes widening and his frown more pronounced.

The man then reached into his pocket and removed his wallet. "Where is it?" he mumbled as he fumbled through it until finally producing a card. "Ah, here it is." He presented the card to Schatten.

"What is this?"

"That man will provide you with prit'near any answer to any question you're lookin' to ask," responded the shop-keeper.

"Wait, what is this thing anyhow?" asked Schatten, cradling the device. "This is no typewriter."

Then the man's demeanor abruptly changed. "Sure it is. But it is no *ordinary* typewriter. It's a doorway . . . and you are the key . . . if you so choose."

Schatten was taken off guard, but before the he could utter another query, the owner preempted him. Pointing to a sign affixed to the wall just inside the doorway, he said, "All sales are final at this store, young man, and the person on the card holds your destiny." Schatten tried to protest, but the old man ushered him out of the shop.

"We're closed. You have to leave."

No sooner had Schatten's feet hit the old wooden porch, that the old man locked the door and drew the shades. Schatten glanced back at the store once more, still holding the merchandise he wanted so desperately to return. But before he took another step, the shopkeeper emerged again and said, "Oh, I almost forgot. When you visit the gentleman on the card, tell him you're there about time. Make certain that you use those exact words or he may not talk to you. Goodbye, young man."

Like a turtle retreating into the safety of its shell, the old man was gone, locked inside his establishment.

"There about time? What the—?"

Schatten shook his head in frustration, annoyed that he hadn't been able to accomplish his mission and get rid of the typewriter. He walked back to his car and opened the trunk, placing the mechanical enigma back inside before closing it. He then removed the card from his pocket and glanced at the name and address.

Dr. Everet Chelston, Professor Emeritus, Harvard University, 218 Stafford Lane, Horton, Mass.

With a sigh, he got back into his car and removed the road atlas he carried with him at all times, despite GPS. He was old-fashioned that way. He chuckled realizing that this is why he'd been drawn to that typewriter.

By his calculations, it was a three-hour drive down the coast. There was no phone number and he found no listing when he tried the web based information services, but he decided to make the trip, nonetheless.

The long drive to Horton, Massachusetts released the bitter memories that Schatten had been suppressing. Despair and anguish pulsed through his veins like a tidal wave of pain. Just over a month ago, his life had come undone within a few hours, and he had aged 100 years. Prior to his Friday meeting with his supervisor, Justin Franks, his confidence had been on the rise. He had put the divorce behind him and was beginning to accept his ex-wife's departure to Phoenix with their son and daughter. But on the bright side, he was drawing royalties from his two books. Since this revenue stream wasn't covered in the divorce settlement, it was all his. He felt as though he had put one over on her and her malicious attorney. But it was a hollow victory, for the war had already been lost, and she had taken everything that mattered.

The one thing that hadn't changed, the thing that provided a stabilizing force in his life, was his job. It provided a constant challenge and allowed him the opportunity to grow as a man and flourish as an engineer. He was second in command, and his boss always had his back. His career was a constant source of pride. The company was growing, and he was a large part of that.

Schatten had arrived at work an hour early that fateful morning, as he did on most days. He unlocked his door and sat in his desk chair and opened his laptop. As he waited for it to boot up, Schatten admired his collection of large-scale WW II fighter aircraft, hung with care from the ceiling of his office with fishing line, when the phone rang at 6:59 a.m. It was Justin Franks, his boss.

"Mike, I need to see you. It's important."

"Sure, be right there," Schatten replied.

No one has a meeting at seven a.m. unless it's a crisis, Schatten thought as he made his way to Justin's office. As he sat in the padded chair in front of his Justin's desk, Schatten noticed immediately that Justin was wearing jeans with a white button-down shirt, deck shoes, and no tie. He never wore such casual attire. Not a word was spoken, as if all the air had been expelled from the room. Justin closed the door, positioned himself in the swivel chair behind the desk, and folded his arms as a frown descended upon his face.

"We've all heard the rumors the past few months, but now it's come true, Mike. The Baker brothers have sold the company and are moving it to Jonesboro, Arkansas. They are laying off everyone, including me—and you. Their old man is probably rolling over in his grave seeing what they've done to the business after they inherited it."

There were no words that would make it better. Schatten trudged away disheartened, disillusioned, insulted, and furious. He had put his heart and soul into the place and garnered nothing in return. In addition, the ridiculous amount of hours spent at the plant had provided his wife the premise for their divorce. Now he had child support, house payments, alimony, rent, utilities, car payments—and no job.

His only sources of income were the dwindling royalties from his two books coupled with a meager cash advance from his publisher for his new book. He was hemorrhaging financially and couldn't stop the bleeding. If he didn't produce the book soon, he'd be ruined.

4
SECRETS

THERE WAS NOTHING DRAMATIC ABOUT Horton, Massachusetts, as Schatten made his way through the town. The town square and main park surrounded the courts building and city hall with a carefully manicured garden. There was a pond in the center, where ducks swam when not begging for food from the residents enjoying their lunches on a myriad of benches.

Small shops were in abundance, predominantly red brick. The stately two-story homes were immaculately landscaped with wonderful gardens and so pristine that each could serve as a travel brochure.

The quaint streets of the sleepy New England town offered no clues as to the dramatic, hidden secrets it harbored. Schatten drove to a park near his destination and sat in his car, trying to fix his position. Looking at the map that he had obtained at the local post office, he found Stafford Lane and walked the six blocks it took to reach the red brick town house at number 218.

The shutters and trim were painted black, and it was a dignified old place, impeccably landscaped and maintained. He opened a black wrought iron gate and slowly walked down the narrow cobblestone pathway and up the three steps to the front door. He grabbed the circular, brass doorknocker and tapped it lightly three times against the ornate wooden door.

He repeated the action with more intensity until the door finally opened, and a small man with glasses emerged. "Can I help you?"

"I'm here about time," Schatten responded, using the phrase offered by the shop owner.

The man looked at him with a curious expression. "I've been expecting you, and time is running out. Come in."

Schatten entered a small hallway with a large grandfather clock steadily ticking, its pendulum swaying rhythmically. On the walls were pictures of various people; many from days gone by, judging from their dress.

"Would you like a cup of tea?" Chelston asked his guest.

"No, I'm fine, thank you," Schatten replied.

"Please," said the host, inviting him into a large room on the left.

The room was decorated in contemporary décor, with one exception—a large wooden desk, replete with a folding top, stood in the right corner. It was obviously an heirloom and was covered with piles of papers in disarray. Bookshelves lined the chamber, bulging with texts of all sizes. The walls were painted dark green, save one that was completely white. It soon became obvious that this was the man's study. There were two high-backed, brown leather chairs facing one another in front of a fireplace and two neutral-colored fabric couches that matched the thick plush carpeting.

His host positioned himself in one chair and offered Schatten the other.

Suddenly, the shrill sound of a teakettle's whistle interrupted. Chelston asked to be excused and left the room, but not before inquiring, "Are you sure you wouldn't care for some tea or anything else to drink?"

"No, thank you," replied Schatten.

Chelston returned shortly, sipping his tea from a china cup in his right hand and holding a saucer in the other. Then he gently placed both on the glass topped table in front of him.

Schatten had left his chair to look at the titles of the many books amassed on a number of shelves.

"You have quite a collection," noted Schatten as he returned to his seat.

"Thank you, I'm an avid reader. As you may have guessed, I am Dr. Everet Chelston, and you are?"

"Schatten, Michael Schatten." He leaned forward to shake hands.

Chelston was the antithesis of what one would envision as the prototypical college professor. He wore a brown, tweed sports coat and gray pants, a white button-down shirt with a rather sedate black tie and brown deck shoes with gray socks. His glasses were of the black, horned-rimmed variety, and his uncombed hair was gray, as were his mustache and bushy eyebrows. The age spots on his hands, wrinkled brow, and neck with circles under the eyes seemed to put his age in the eighties, but he was in good physical condition and very spry.

"I know that you have questions about the typewriter, but I feel it's—"

"How did you know I—" Schatten was sure he hadn't even mentioned the device.

Chelston raised his hand to stop him. "It's important to give the background, so before you pose your questions, please indulge me." Chelston smiled. "It has some peculiar traits, doesn't it?"

"Yes, yes it does."

Schatten couldn't put his finger on it, but it was as though Chelston knew exactly who he was and why he was there. But the professor put him at ease like a grandfather telling his grandson an old tale.

"It was born out of a highly classified project; several projects, actually. But before we go any further, I must have your promise that you will not divulge to anyone, for any reason, what I am about to reveal."

Intrigued Schatten replied, "Yes sir, of course."

Chelston picked up a small remote control and dimmed the lights before activating a projector from the wall's interior above the fireplace, which cast the image of several individuals.

"The chairs swivel," said Chelston, turning to face the color photo projection on the white wall opposite the fireplace.

"During the World War II, I was a young student working for the university while pursuing my doctorate."

Chelston fumbled through his pockets and retrieved a laser pointer.

"I was enlisted by one of my professors to join a highly secretive project. The picture before you shows some of my fellow researchers. That's me, third on the right," he said training the laser on his likeness to emphasize the point. "Do any of them catch your eye?"

Schatten studied the grainy picture. It showed a line of ten men in casual dress posing in front of various pieces of old electronic equipment, lining numerous laboratory tables. Schatten quickly panned the gallery of faces presented, but none of them stood out.

"Take a good look at the gentleman on the far right," Chelston said, pointing. "I assume you have seen him before?"

As Schatten leaned forward in his chair, it was suddenly obvious why Chelston had singled out this individual.

Chelston smiled. "I take it you recognize that person now?"

Speechless, Schatten nodded. It was Albert Einstein.

"Working alongside him, on this project, was the most enlightening and humbling experience of my life." Chelston paused for a moment as if lost in his memory of the great scientist. "Einstein was fascinated by the concept of time. No, let me rephrase that, he was obsessed with time. Although known in scientific circles for theories such as relativity, he devoted countless hours speculating about time. When the United States government approached him with an unlimited budget to explore the possibility of altering time, he found the idea irresistible.

It was explained to the great physicist that the goal of the project was to see if some of his theories could be proven in the laboratory and then lend themselves to the mission at hand. Controlled and funded by the military, the real goal was to win the war at all costs and covertly create a new advanced weapon . . . a time machine."

Schatten had to swallow a laugh. A time machine? Was this man joking?

"The leadership understood that achieving this monumental endeavor, rivaling any of man's past accomplishments, could only be realized by enlisting the most fertile intellects in the world. If this could be done, it might be possible to rewrite history and not even fight a war. If they could eliminate Hitler before he came to power, the world might avoid another conflict."

"Revisionist history to the nth degree," said Schatten, willing to play along for a little bit.

"More like a revisionist future," said Chelston solemnly. "The military viewed Einstein as a possible security risk due to his political leanings. And it didn't help that he was a pacifist. Although he had initially lent his name and helped draft a letter to the President addressing how it was theoretically possible to create an atomic weapon, he did not actively participate in building it. You may recall that the code name of that endeavor became the Manhattan Project. So they theorized that he would reject anything associated with weapons development. With this mindset, the military disingenuously conveyed to the great scientist that the fruits of his labor would be the creation of purely defensive devices that would save countless lives. As part of the illusion, the scientists were given free reign, and the experiments conceived were endless, since there were no boundaries in their research."

"And these experiments produced a typewriter?" Schatten couldn't hold back his impatience.

"You are too impatient, my young friend. The project was given the code name AST, which stood for the Alteration of Space and Time. Only a select few even knew what the acronym meant. The participants were but pawns in a race to develop the ultimate device to make the United States invincible, both militarily and politically."

Chelston paused and sighed, as if he'd arrived at a crossroads in his story that would explain everything.

"But to ensure that everything we accomplished was steered in the direction of the time machine, the commanding general planted a mole into our group of researchers, who reported directly to him. It was more highly classified than even the Manhattan Project. It was one of the first 'Black' programs. Not even congress knew of its existence. Both the Army and Navy used the development of the atomic bomb, as a smokescreen to cipher off exorbitant amounts of capital to fund this new venture. There was no traceability or accountability, since the project never existed on paper."

"What does altering time have to do with the typewriter? Are you sure that we're discussing my antiquated machine?" asked Schatten.

"Your typewriter is one of a few remaining gadgets developed from that project."

"What makes a simple typewriter a Time Machine?"

"Energy. Tremendous amounts of energy. Generating such power became a project unto itself. For this, we needed the top mind in the world; an expert who understood electromagnetic fields and how to engender and harness them."

Chelston leaned forward and pointed at the picture. "Now I want you to concentrate on the individual in the picture on the far left. Do you recognize that man?"

Schatten peered at the picture intently. "No, who is he?"

Chelston smiled. "That man is Nikola Tesla. He died January 7, 1943, and it was a great loss to us all. He worked on the project for about a year and a half. Without his effort, and his brilliant mind, nothing would have been accomplished."

Chelston smiled again. "Take another look. Do you see that Tesla and Einstein were at opposite sides of the picture. This was by choice, for the two had their differences, to put it mildly."

"Fine. I guess they worked together alright?"

"They did, my friend, they did. The experiments Tesla produced in our lab were breathtaking. In fact, he left most of us scratching our heads as to how his devices worked. Tesla once provided enough energy to run an entire town with a generator located hundreds of miles away, using no wires. He laid the plans for a death ray to annihilate any enemy and tried to sell it to any country that would listen as the end-all weapon to prevent future wars. The man was unique and gifted, and his work was watched keenly by the US military and security services. In fact, all his notes and experiments were seized by the government after the war."

"But not the typewriter?"

"I am getting there, my friend. Most of our other experiments were unsuccessful, resulting from the lack of technology in three vital areas; one was materials, two was electronics, and three was computing power."

"What do mean exactly?" asked Schatten.

"The time machine required Tesla to provide enormous energy, which generated enormous heat and melted the mechanical components like bearings and other highly stressed areas."

"So what types of materials did you develop?" asked Schatten.

"Ceramics, high strength steel, and titanium alloys. Materials that no one knew much about until the advent of high-altitude spy planes and the space program decades later."

"Look, this is all fascinating, but what does it have to do with the typewriter?" Schatten pressed.

"Well, there is a small black box under the keyboard. Did you ever notice it?"

Chelston pushed away several papers exposing a wireless keyboard laying on the table, which he placed on his lap. His fingers began typing as he pulled up a three-dimensional picture of the typewriter, deftly projected it on the wall and rotated it to expose the underside. The keyboard interfaced with a hidden computer that housed all his data in a huge inventory of files.

Focusing the laser on a small rectangular black box, Chelston said, "That rascal there is your answer."

"What is it?"

"A piece of electronic wizardry," replied Chelston.

"What does it do?"

"It provides a wireless link to the rest of the system."

"The rest of the system? Can you possibly be more cryptic?" Schatten threw his hands up in the air in surrender.

"You really need to work on your patience, Mr. Schatten." Chelston shook his head as if to chastise a petulant child. "Having resolved the power and material issues, we turned our attention to revamping our antiquated electronic designs, requiring huge amounts of space for even the simplest devices. Our rooms of electronic equipment, used to run the various experiments, if designed with present day technology could be stored on the head of a pin. The project was saved through an insertion of technology introduced from origins that even to this day remain a mystery."

"No one knew?" asked a dubious Schatten.

"One did; a mysterious individual introduced as Colonel Taylor. He appeared one afternoon in our conference room with devices that would not reveal themselves in the public eye for twenty years or more. He placed four large manila envelopes on the table and said, 'Gentlemen I want you to keep these items and reverse engineer and adapt them for this project. You have unlimited manpower to accomplish this. I want you to patent everything here and integrate it into the private sector. And I want this accomplished yesterday.' That said, he just walked out, and no one ever saw him again."

"What was in the envelopes?"

"The fundamentals of fiber optics, miniaturized circuitry and microprocessors."

"Back then?"

"Indeed, back then. Several top technical captains of the industry were present to review the description of the various enigmatic devices and to offer how to recreate them in the lab. We were told that they would gain exclusive rights to the technology, once they had developed and refined it for the present experiments."

Chelston paused yet again, shooting a look at Schatten that promised a final revelation.

"Rumors that these innovations stemmed from crashed alien spacecraft spread like wildfire. Security was heightened, and the rumor mill was quashed as microphones were installed throughout the complex. Those that engaged in such speculation were chastised, fined, or dismissed. The only brainstorming allowed was on the task at hand, not the origins of the technological windfall."

"Forgive me, Professor, but are you saying that today's electronics are based upon alien designs?" Once again Schatten suppressed the urge to laugh out loud.

"I would scoff also, had I not been there. But I swear I am not exaggerating."

"Okay, I'll bite. Please go on."

"There was one last imposing obstacle to be addressed. They knew it would be impossible to control the intricacies of each experiment without an electronic brain to aid in the calculations and provide data storage and the cataloging of each step. So they developed a calculating device. It was not called a computer but was given the designation of SAMCD—Secret Assimilation and Mathematical Computational Device—which they affectionately referred to as SAM. Work began in earnest to construct the device, which initially consisted of rooms filled with bulky circuit boxes. The brightest electronic engineers from both the academic world and industry worked tirelessly to integrate the new technology afforded them into a revolutionary design. And part of the process was to create a device as a means of communicating between man and machine."

"The typewriter finally rears its ugly head," said Schatten.

"The typewriter was selected as the means of data input, since it was simple, contained all of the letters and numbers we needed, and was a device known to all. Five would be modified to ensure that backups were available, should one or more fail during test trials."

"So my typewriter is one of the five?"

"Yes. As the space required for the SAM computer began to shrink and the efficiency, power, and speed of the unit began to increase exponentially, programs were written to link it to the typewriters. Finally, the SAM and the typewriters were coupled to the massive electrical field generator to serve as the control mechanism."

Schatten interrupted. "Excuse me, but are you telling me that this was the genesis of the modern computer?"

"Yes," replied the professor.

"But I've followed the history of the computer through the 1940s to 50s and the related punch card era. The chronology of what you're discussing should have put the process of development far ahead of the actual historical timeline."

"My boy, the things accomplished in that laboratory were astounding and so was the pace. Unfortunately, much of the innovation and achievements were classified and never shared with the outside world. Our computer would not be duplicated for decades by the private sector. None of the secrets and insights learned in our lab were passed on because there was an air of paranoia, unprecedented in the annals of war. The Russian and German intelligence networks were formidable. Why, even the Manhattan Project was not immune to the tentacles of both these organizations. Our project was even more highly classified, and so security was even tighter. No one had a phone that wasn't tapped or any correspondence that wasn't read by security before it was sent anywhere. The word secret, my friend," Chelston pointed at the image on the wall, "was invented for this. But getting back to your question regarding the evolution of the computer . . . our engineers developed direct input between the keyboard and the SAM, like today's machines."

"So the black box," said Schatten, also indicating the figure on the wall, "is connected to a computer, wirelessly?"

"Yes, which is coupled to Tesla's massive power generator. The thought was that anyone could be sent back in time and recovered from anywhere just by typing in certain commands."

"Professor, I think I'll have that tea now."

5
EINSTEIN'S SALVATION

SCHATTEN PACED TRYING TO DIGEST everything. When the professor brought the tea, Schatten took a long sip as he sat back down.

"All right, Professor, I take it your project met everyone's expectations, otherwise the typewriters would have been scrapped."

"No, in fact it was disastrous."

"Come again?" said Schatten caught off guard, almost spilling his tea.

"The day came when we all convened to demonstrate the system," Chelston continued. "The immense field generator was activated and the building shook. But the square block of aluminum which was to vanish in time and retrieved failed to disappear. The military was apoplectic."

"Unbeknownst to the others, Paul Steiner, the mole I'd mentioned earlier, was given daily project reports on the atomic bomb. They were in a race with the Manhattan Project to end the war. So instead of using objects and transitioning to lab rats, the military now demanded that sacrificial human guinea pigs be used. They gave Steiner an ultimatum, show something tangible within thirty days or the project would be canceled.

"Steiner's first demonstration to give the military some-thing concrete was an experiment in which a navy destroyer was modified with huge magnetic coils and energized by one of Tesla's portable power generators. The Navy hoped to create an enormous electrical field around the ship to make it disappear on radar.

Instead, the ship completely vanished and then rematerialized, resulting in the ghastly deaths of twenty sailors."

"You're discussing the Philadelphia Experiment," said Schatten, feeling as though he was inexplicably corroborating the story. "What happened exactly?"

Chelston seemed pleasantly surprised that Schatten had recognized what he was talking about. "That's excellent, yes, that's correct. Apparently, the crew and their ship went forward into time and reappeared some hours later.

"The men had been displaced relative to the vessel during their exposure to the intense field and ended up occupying the same space as the ship's structure. Bodies, arms, skulls, and legs became fused with steel. It's an image one doesn't forget.

"This was followed by more tragedy in our lab as a volunteer, PVT Dennis Cole, was sent back in time but returned with the hardware that accompanied him grotesquely fused to his body like the sailors aboard the destroyer. To see men die like that is . . ."

Chelston had to collect himself.

"Einstein was so horrified that he immediately terminated his association with the project and just walked away, leaving all his diaries and notes. The time machine concept was scrapped, and the project was on the verge of termination when it was unwittingly saved by Einstein himself."

"Are we close to why the typewriter does what it does?"

Chelston ignored him. "Upon Einstein's sudden disassociation and departure, the lead position fell to Paul Steiner, whose budget was now slashed. But Einstein would inadvertently provide salvation. Pouring over the great man's notes, Steiner came upon an incredible file. In it, Einstein was covertly experimenting on his off hours. He sought to use Tesla's source of unlimited power as a way of proving a phenomenon he had speculated about for years. It involved the concept of the doppelgänger, the creation of an exact duplicate of another person or object. He was obsessed by the concept stemming from his actual encounter with his duplicate. In his notes he claimed that he had observed his doppelgänger purchase candy from a bakery and simply vanish into a crowd as he pursued him. He never shared his theory but speculated that the phenomena could only be caused by a massive gravitational field resulting from sunspots, a meteor, comet or asteroid coming too close to the earth in short duration."

"And Tesla's energy device!" shouted Schatten, beginning to piece together the puzzle.

"Precisely, dear boy. He equated it to the effect of throwing a small pebble into still water. The stone and its reflection would meet as it entered the water. After the rippling effect subsided, the surface would return to a calm state."

"So, I inadvertently created a series of these doppelgängers?"

"Yes, now let's fill in the rest of the puzzle. We're in the homestretch. Steiner's imagination went wild as he saw a new potential for our project. He postulated that if this theory was true, they could create duplicate beings for short periods of time, beings that could theoretically be given missions, after which they simply vanished without a trace. They would be the perfect disposable soldiers.

"When Steiner revealed this concept to the other researchers, all understood why Einstein had never shared this outrageous theory. During a brainstorming session, the group theorized that our powerful field generator could indeed provide the means to create the distortion to allow the future, past, and present to merge. When this happened, a duplicate character might be created. But simply creating a character was meaningless unless we could control his actions to perform a specific task. The team conjectured that if a storyline could be composed regarding a specific character created by their time distortion, he could hypothetically be programmed to carry out any activity they desired. Accomplishing this would require an interface with the SAM computer to turn a story into reality."

Schatten was beginning to see a connection to everything, including his characters.

"The group, now reenergized by this concept, worked tirelessly around the clock. Then, finally, we were able to try our first experiment. We reasoned that this character must be based upon an actual person and that the characteristics of that individual must be downloaded into the SAM's memory. The story was carefully composed by the group and then typed on one of the typewriters."

"So, after reading Einstein's notes, you knew exactly how to simply conjure up a living, breathing human that acts like a robot that you control?" Schatten couldn't fathom what he'd heard.

"Well, it wasn't simple, by any means. We tried the experiment numerous times over a one-week period, but nothing happened. So we went back to Einstein's notes. One of them simply read, *One must initiate and terminate the time distortion seamlessly*. Finally, one of the scientists understood its significance. He postulated that the character must be given a beginning and an end. The character must be provided an entrance into reality and then be given an exit so that the time continuum could go back to a stable condition analogous to the still pond that Einstein had described previously."

"So, what I did was unwittingly create real beings that acted out my storylines?"

"Yes."

"But I didn't even know about the send button. Why did the typewriter automatically send it?"

"Well, we opened the send button to allow everything you wrote to come true for a limited time. This way, you could see the power of the device and have a feel for what it could do. We could hardly have this conversation if you hadn't seen it for yourself. Otherwise, who in their right mind would believe it? We monitored your machine to ensure that your sagas and characters were harmless if they were brought to life for brief periods."

"How could you monitor my machine?"

"Let's just say we have the technology to do so and leave it at that."

Schatten wanted to object but Chelston's facial expression signaled that this was not negotiable.

"Now, a character could be created in the mind of whoever was at the keyboard, and this profile could in turn be sent to the SAM computer, which fused with the field generator to provide the energy required. But the character must be based upon a real subject, thus eliminating the concept that the system could play God and create new people from nothing but imagination. They started by generating characters based upon the individuals in our group. A file with all the physical characteristics for each volunteer was downloaded into the memory of the SAM computer. Once this was accomplished, a short storyline was created for each character. The tale was simple, and each story took place in the lab. The duplicate would walk through the outside door to the lab, proceed to the water cooler, fill up a paper cup, drink the contents, crumple and discard the cup. They would exit through the door, ending the storyline.

"The same script was repeated for each new character. We were careful to limit the time of exposure to the magnetic field of the person being copied, since no one understood the short or long-term effects. In each case, the computer then selected the individual from its memory that most closely approximated the character in the storyline. It then extracted the amount of energy from that person required to create the doppelgänger."

"So all my characters were based upon real people? Who were some of them?"

"John Prescott was David Klinger from Oakdale, California, and Ms. Adams was Gail Fuget from Mason City, Iowa. We have a listing of everyone you created and their counterparts. I can print it out if you'd like."

Schatten shook his head.

"That's not necessary, thank you, but what happens to them once the day's storyline has been completed?"

"I think you found that out on your own. They disappear. The electromagnetic field generating the characters also has an effect on the human brain. People who are exposed to the replicas have their memories altered to some degree. Most have no recollection about the people after the storyline is completed. We designed it that way to ensure that only the actions were remembered and not the artificial beings."

"I've heard the term doppelgänger before but never quite understood what it meant. You mean the typewriter can create an exact duplicate of any person or thing?"

"Yes, to put it simply. But in true terms, the entire system performs the miracle, since the typewriter is only one component."

"So all the characters I created were already in the computer's memory? I find that an unbelievable coincidence."

"Yes, it would be, if it weren't for the fact that a profile of almost every living person on earth or contemporary thing has been amassed inside the SAM's memory. The intelligence agencies and the military saw to that. They provided all the information, as well as the staff, to download and maintain it. The process continues to this day. It provides them with a centralized database to track almost everyone or thing on the face of the earth."

Schatten's mind was spinning.

"So the computer searches its memory for the person or thing that you wish to recreate. But what if the individual that you're trying to copy lives in Tibet . . . how does your contraption reach out and touch that person? Do you have to physically bring them here?"

"No, my boy, you could say *we* go to *them*. As you stated, we really do reach out and touch them, wherever they happen to be. Thanks to Tesla, the field generator can project or extract the required energy from the far corners of the globe. It bounces its signal off the atmosphere. Tesla demonstrated the concept by generating a huge electromagnetic field in his lab here and directing it to a remote spot in the Swiss Alps. It provided the power to light the entire town of Berkondaul for some 48 hours. As I stated previously, the man was a genius, he even created AC current. He completed his work on the device we currently operate just before he died. Then we used his notes to enlarge the device and improve the process even further. The field would lock onto the targeted individual and draw just enough energy from them and use it to create the duplicate wherever we pleased.

"The people, whose lives unwittingly served as the basis for the artificial beings, would be returned to their mundane existences unscathed, without any knowledge of what had occurred. Or so we thought. But this was identity theft to the extreme.

"The action of creating duplicate beings drastically changed Steiner and our group. We no longer viewed this as the means to create robotic soldiers. Instead, we all agreed to strive for a high moral standard in the use of such power and refrain from its abuse. But of course, this goal would be tainted by the objectives of the military."

"Exactly how did you establish the two-week time limit on the doppelgängers?"

"There was one caveat to the supposed harmlessness of creating the characters. When we tried to lengthen the stay of one of our creations, they found the lab assistant who served as our model slumped in the corner of a room, near death. We rushed the individual to the hospital, where he regained consciousness. He said that all at once, he could see his duplicate in his mind and was suddenly aware of everything the character had done. It felt as if his life was draining from him."

"Wow, so not only does the device provide the means to steal the identity of anyone you please, with the real possibility that the people who serve as the host for the duplicate could get blamed for its actions, but it is also potentially lethal." Schatten was appalled by this last disclosure.

"Sadly, yes," confessed the professor.

It finally dawned on Schatten how very dangerous the device really was.

"With this shocking revelation, the doppelgänger was immediately terminated along with the storyline on which we had been working. It was only then that someone understood the note in Einstein's remarks: *Beware the Chi!* Now it was apparent that Einstein had referred to the Chinese concept of Chi, or the life force within all of us. When the character was allowed to remain active for too long, it would start to drain the life force from its host . . . and not only that, it would begin to meld with the person upon whom it was based. If left unchecked, the doppelgänger would become the actual individual, *killing* the host. Moreover, once the maximum time threshold had been passed, even if the duplicate was terminated in time and ceased to exist, its actions would be permanently embedded into the memory of the individual who served as the host. This meant that after a certain time period, the actions of the duplicate creation were not covert by any means, for now, the host individual would become a witness to all its actions."

"So what—"

Chelston seemed to know what Schatten was going to ask and interrupted. "You will be happy to know that the lab assistant recovered fully in roughly one week with no discernible lasting effects, other than the memory of the duplicate's activities."

"What are the boundaries for this thing? Can you make your characters go back in time?"

"We never got that far, so the answer is no. Everything is contemporary with every character living in the present," responded Chelston.

"That's not true at all," shouted Schatten. "I created a Viking vessel along with its crew, a whaling ship with its full complement, and a WWII P-61 Black Widow fighter."

"Michael, your Vikings were contemporary college students who enacted raids as part of their historical club and to get extra credit. They built their ship as part of their history class project. They have permission by the communities to visit homes along the way and leave the owner a fifty-dollar gift certificate as a reward. The whaler was a restoration from the New England Maritime Museum traveling back up the eastern seaboard from a Florida regatta. The P-61 fighter was a restoration from a collector in Texas, who regularly flies his aircraft around the US for various events," Chelston said, smiling.

"So the Allosaurus was a non-starter," remarked Schatten.

"Again, it wasn't contemporary, it wasn't tangible. The pirate ship you tried to conjure up failed to match any such vessel in the SAM's database that was seaworthy."

"So you watched me from the beginning, haven't you? What would have happened if I had done something sinister with the machine?"

"I think you know the answer. The machine would have been turned off and we would have retrieved it."

Schatten shrugged.

"In the beginning," Chelston went on, "this came with an unlimited potential for good. Just imagine if an artificial person could perform a job too dangerous for any normal individual, like running into a burning building or handling toxic waste; perhaps testing out serums or serving as an astronaut. There were countless experiments yet to be conducted, but no one in the military shared our enthusiasm, and the project was abruptly terminated."

Schatten found that hard to believe. "Just like that?"

Chelston nodded.

"Well, events happened at that time that would overshadow our efforts. Hitler and his henchmen were dead, Germany had surrendered, and the Manhattan Project suddenly gained notoriety as the two atomic bombs were dropped on Japan that led to that nation's capitulation. Their endeavors were no longer driven by a pressing requirement, and the goals of the project were skewed.

"Steiner still championed their cause as the Russians emerged as the new threat, but it fell on deaf ears. Not surprisingly, the parts of the project that still interested the military were our massive computer and power generator. Funds were given to continue its development to see if its full potential could be realized. The funding was slashed for everything else. The typewriting units were to be shipped to the British as part of various technology exchanges between the two allies with the provision that they would fund the continued research and provide detailed documentation of all experiments conducted. Four of the five functioning typewriters were sent to London by air transport, but tragically, the aircraft crashed somewhere around the town of Salisbury, England."

Schatten knew this was not the end of the story, but he never imagined it was about to thrust him into the Twilight Zone.

6
THE OFFER

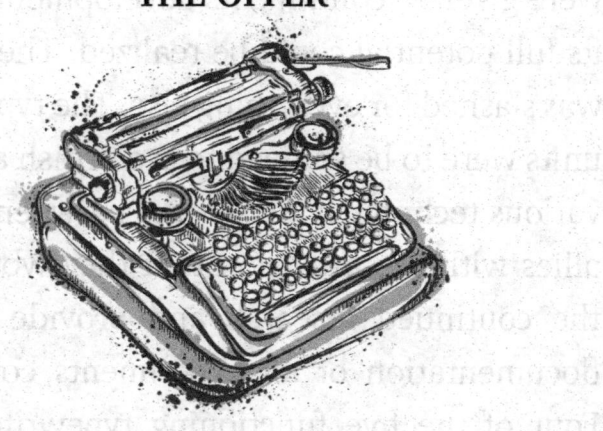

THE PROFESSOR ROSE TO HIS FEET. "Michael, let's get down to why you're here, beyond your own curiosity. You have demonstrated that you know how the device works, you have a feel for its idiosyncrasies, and now you know the history behind it. How would you like to work for me for a few weeks? We would like to put your unique talents to use."

Schatten was dumbfounded and stood ready to leave.

"I'm sorry, Professor, but I really have wasted enough time with this gizmo of yours. I promised to have a copy of my manuscript on my publisher's desk by the end of next month. I'm sorry, but I really have to get back to work."

"We would like to offer you an advance of $100,000, tax-free cash, for a week's work . . . using your typewriter," replied Chelston, cavalierly. "Unless your bank account is already bulging."

"Who are *we*?"

"The few remnants of the researchers that created your device."

Schatten was stunned. He did a quick inventory of his financial situation. He had rolled the dice coming to New England, using what little capital he had, to finish his book with no guarantee of success.

What Chelston was offering was a king's ransom. Even if the book was brilliant, it wouldn't ease his monetary situation.

"What would I have to do?"

"Write a simple script based upon someone else's storyline."

"Who's storyline?"

"Someone in possession of a device similar to yours," said Chelston.

"I thought you said that the other typewriters were lost when the plane went down?"

"I only said that the plane crashed. But let me complete the saga, from where we left off."

Schatten sat back down.

"Every inch of the wreckage had been searched. Although two of the four units were destroyed by flames, the others remained missing. The only saving grace was that the US researchers had kept one typewriter for themselves as a link with their UK counterparts. It was that unit that you now possess. But this device is unique, for it has the ability to monitor the outputs from the other machines."

"What exactly does that mean, Professor?"

"At the outset, the researchers had equipped this machine with a Teletype that would immediately print out anything being written and identify the source. Over the years, a computer and laser printer replaced the Teletype, and upgraded to track the exact location of any unit transmitting a signal. Several years passed before the two missing units began transmitting.

"One was traced to a woman in France who was using it to write cookbooks. A team was immediately dispatched, and the unit was purchased from her at a lucrative price, making the woman happy and none the wiser. She purchased it from an antique shop in Salisbury. The owner of the store relented that he was a member of the local volunteer fire brigade that had rushed to the crash scene to extinguish the blaze and search for survivors. He had removed the two machines, unaware of their significance. He smuggled them back to his store but was unable to identify the individual who had purchased the second item.

"The transmissions were eventually traced to an area outside Salisbury, England. It was unclear as to who owned the unit . . . until a series of books were published mirroring the content of the material coming from the rogue typewriter. The initial offerings were spy novels in the Ian Fleming genre and so implausible that there was never any anxiety that they could become reality.

"But it was the next generation of stories that created concerns. These tales were 'techno thrillers,' as the colloquial term was coined, involving stories of military exploits employing state-of-the-art warfare technology. They exhibited much more intricate detail and moved closer to achieving the threshold of plausibility, giving rise to the fear that once received, the SAM computer might make the storyline fact."

Schatten was confused. "Who's the guy you're talking about?"

"Demetri Karamov," replied the professor.

"The Russian Tom Clancy?"

"Yes, I see you are familiar with the man's work."

"Yeah, I even read some of his novels."

"What was your overall impression?" asked Chelston.

"Long, involved, with really intricate detail."

A light was beginning to dawn in Schatten's mind.

"What's his history, and why is he suddenly a threat?" asked Schatten.

"Karamov has a sordid past, working for the KGB for years before retiring to become an author. Many of his most notable works corresponded to the timeframe after the typewriter became active. This was significant in that the plots around which his stories unfolded all came to pass, after my group began receiving signals. The novels' settings were localized, mostly in remote areas of the Russian landscape, and the KGB and Soviet government covered up the events that resulted. I shouldn't use the acronym KGB any longer since it was replaced by the FSB, but old habits die hard. The stories involved a litany of subjects including insurrections, downed aircrafts, naval skirmishes, and scuffling between elements of the British, US, and Soviet militaries. But the common thread was that they occurred benignly, always with the main character, his James Bond equivalent agent Uri Kulof, prevailing. Since world peace was never compromised, he was allowed to continue unabated."

"If you knew who he was, why not just stop him and retrieve the unit?" asked Schatten.

"First, Karamov became famous, and he had his own security force living around Salisbury. Secondly, our modest monitoring program was secretly funded but officially unfunded and an embarrassment to many circles in the US government. We are not connected to the security or military arm of any of the services that could assassinate or capture the man or take the device by force. Can you imagine trying to explain to the CIA director that we require an agent to assassinate a world-famous author because he was using a device developed to change history that we manufactured but were stupid enough to let fall into enemy hands?"

"Yeah, I see your point," replied Schatten. "But if he's ex-KGB, why didn't he sell it to the Russians?"

"To put it simply, he was driven by power, dear boy. Why give away the genie in the lamp? With no budget and with no manpower available outside the inner circle of those involved in the project from its inception, there was little that

Revisionist Future

could be done to halt the man's activities. As long as humanity was safe, there was no issue."

"I fail to see my relevance in all this," remarked Schatten.

"Karamov is now attempting to expand the scope of his activities and include the use of nuclear weapons. Seemingly not content with the fame and accolades reserved for a noted author, he was striving to push the limits of his stolen technology. He was formulating a plan to place himself in the position of absolute authority in a new world order. As was the case with most wealthy individuals, riches were meaningless unless accompanied by power. He would orchestrate his own ascension in league with a diabolical mix of disgruntled military, terrorists, and underworld types. The outcome would be paid by the lives of millions of innocent people. His creation would be ghastly and result in a world uninhabitable in many corners of the globe. Those that survived would be subjugated by a totalitarian order."

"How do you know this?"

"We've only seen bits and pieces of the puzzle but enough to recognize the picture," added

Chelston. "He has been laying the groundwork for months, so to speak."

"Wait a minute. When I tried to inject myself into the story that I was writing, I couldn't do it. Nothing ever happened. How could *he* possibly do it?" asked Schatten.

"He shouldn't be able to, but he's pushing this technology into areas that we never intended. Quite frankly, he may be able to do things with the system that even surprises us. I would have never thought it possible, but I cannot risk the chance . . . and neither can you. If he can't accomplish these things, then nothing happens, and the story is rejected in its entirety, and life goes on. But if, by the slim chance, he has found a way to take this system to the next level . . ."

Chelston abruptly leaned forward in his chair, intently stared at Schatten, and stated, "Which leads us to your presence. Michael, we sensed that you were the type of individual who wanted to know what your device was and that you would not exploit it for any ill-gotten gain. But not everyone is blessed with your integrity, which is why we need your help. We need you to write for us. We need you to stop him by defusing his plot."

"How are you monitoring his story if I have the only other unit?"

The professor smiled, "Very astute, Michael. Remember the typewriter we obtained from the French woman? We upgraded that unit with the same capabilities as yours once we brought it back to the lab."

Schatten shook his head. This was all beginning to feel surreal. He didn't want to be drawn in further.

"First of all, what proof do you have that Karamov is a main character in his own story?"

"Because one of the main characters is clearly a self-portrait, down to the scar on his left wrist."

"Won't the system automatically find someone similar that meets the description and not allow him to be a part of the plot? I couldn't even touch my characters, let alone talk to them, so how could he expect to accomplish this?" asked Schatten.

"He shouldn't and that's what's disturbing."

"How could Karamov possibly understand all the idiosyncrasies of the system?

"We believe that he also found one of the manuals that accompanied each device," replied Chelston.

"You're joking. There were manuals with each machine that explained everything? Wouldn't that be a major security breach?"

"In hindsight, yes," responded Chelston, clearly embarrassed. "We assumed that the Army would guard it closely. Obviously, we were wrong."

"So, he submits his manuscript all at once. When would Karamov know whether or not his manuscript was accepted or rejected?"

"The system is designed for the SAM to scrutinize the storyline in one week; seven days. Then it's either rejected or accepted."

"So, after the submittal, Karamov will only know after the week was up that it was rejected or accepted?" asked Schatten.

"Not necessarily. If the computer was ahead of schedule in its review cycle, he might hear sooner, but he must resubmit any corrections before the week is up. The approval cycle is precisely one week regardless of the number of resubmittals."

"So how exactly would he know if his storyline was rejected?"

"There is small red light on the side of the keyboard signifying rejection and a green indicating acceptance by the SAM."

"Could he know what the mistakes were?"

"Yes, he will also receive an error message, if he has a printer plugged in."

"But he wouldn't know whether anyone altered his plot, right?"

"He will when he sees the changes after the rejection."

"Okay, then following that logic, if I destroy his plot and the SAM approves the storyline, the only thing he'll see is the green light. He would be blind to my alteration, right?"

"Very perceptive. Yes, Karamov would be blind to that possibility. So you see, you'll have the advantage."

"What will prevent him from just undoing the changes and resubmitting the story?"

"One of the rules is that no change can be made twice. That also applies to the submission of a storyline. Once it's submitted, it will be rejected if it's resubmitted without changes from the original submission."

"Is Karamov aware that you know what he's doing?" asked Schatten.

"He has an inflated ego which allows him to think that he is invulnerable, regardless."

"So when do you assume that he will start submitting the entire story?" asked Schatten.

"We feel that it is imminent. That is why we wanted you here, now. We want you to be ready so that when he does so, you can defeat his scheme. From the time it's submitted in its entirety to the time it comes to fruition will be a period of one week—no more, no less."

"Surely you have someone on your staff responsible for changing or editing stories. Why can't that person deal with Karamov?" asked Schatten.

"Unfortunately, that person died recently. He was our resident writer who served as the person responsible for editing storylines. We called him the Unwriter." Chelston chuckled. "He was both an engineer and an accomplished journalist. We see *you* in that same vein."

"So you're asking me to replace him and take on a writer of Karamov's ilk?"

"Well, yes."

"So what would have happened if I never brought back the typewriter to the shop?"

"We would have called you and asked to set up an appointment to speak to you. Do you know how easy it was to obtain your phone number from my friends in the NSA?"

"If I agree, how will I receive his work?"

"You will be provided a computer and a printer, and both will be connected to your typewriter. When the main computer signals that the storyline has been received, your computer will receive the entire manuscript. At that same moment, the printer will print out the entire text. From the time when you receive the complete manuscript you will have seven calendar days to defeat the plot."

"But what if the book is 800 pages or more? How can I read through that much text and still write my own counter? I couldn't possibly write an equivalent amount in a week."

"No, you don't understand, my boy. You won't be required to write another book. You merely interject passages in key locations that will negate what he's trying to accomplish. They must fit seamlessly into his storyline. You will be required to write concisely, just enough to ensure that his plot is implausible, or plausible but harmless. Then the original text—with your additions—will be immediately rejected by the SAM. The other scenario would be to alter the plot such that you take it into a direction where there are no dire consequences. You can undo what he has done and turn the story into a benign series of actions that have no effect on the world at large. But you must be careful to interface cleanly with his text. You can't just blatantly compose that everyone went home and lived happily ever after. That would violate the protocol established for submitting changes. That was done to prevent easy sabotage. You'll have to do some research and provide details that will be unimpeachable by the main computer's logic. You'll simply write quality, not quantity, to defeat his plot."

"So you're saying that if his plot was to fly a plane into a building, I could ground the aircraft before it took off or land it before it did any harm?"

"Yes, you can elect to go many different directions to defuse whatever he is attempting."

"This guy has access to documents and data that I couldn't even imagine and he might be discussing technology that I haven't even heard of," responded Schatten.

"Well, there I can help level the playing field," replied Chelston.

"How?"

"I will give you an access code to connect to a highly classified system used for counter-intelligence. It shows the vulnerabilities of almost every weapons system imaginable. It will reveal flaws and give recommendations to defeat or disable most foreign weaponry. It also will offer a complete rundown on all known technology."

"I can just plug in from any outlet, and no one will care?" asked Schatten.

"With the passwords and small modem, you will be given, you will basically have carte blanche access with no traceability."

"And if someone *does* discover my presence?"

"Well, that is a minimal risk. Should that contingency arise, I'm afraid that you would be on your own. This project is known only to a select few."

"Whose site is it?"

"It's run by naval intelligence and the NSA," said Chelston.

"What? Are you telling me you can just hack into two of the most classified organizations in the entire world?"

"No hacker would be allowed to access a source such as this. I'm afraid I can't explain beyond that point, but if you must use a coined term, it would be akin to a back door and a quite camouflaged one, even to the most astute. Remember, our team was involved with the creation of the first computer . . . and developing code. But I will not say more than that on that topic."

"Fine. So continue, please."

"You will have access through a surreptitious mode constructed by the person who conceived the programming. It was essentially a spare key, so to speak, circumventing the security measures and allowing a single, almost undetectable, tunnel into the inner sanctum of the most secure."

Chelston walked over to his desk and opened the top left-hand drawer. He removed a packet and handed it to Schatten.

"This takes you step by step through each firewall and every security level for the database I just described. You will be utilizing the small black box on the underside of the typewriter for everything that is required. Inside that mysterious little device are the solid-state electronics that will not only interface wirelessly with the SAM computer but will also help you to enter the classified database."

"How will it help me with the database access?" asked Schatten as he reluctantly took the packet.

"It will simulate a government access card. The system will never know the difference, and it will be seamless to you, so you needn't worry."

Then Chelston walked over to the corner of the room, picked up a box, and returned to place it at Schatten's feet.

"Inside, you will find the instructions to assemble the system required to accomplish the mission. You will find a laptop computer, modem/router, and printer. Paper is provided to start you out, but you will require more. The equipment provided will plug into the typewriter. The computer will record all that you type and what the unit is receiving. The only time that you must use the typewriter keyboard is to send the script in its final form. To repeat, if it is accepted, a green light will illuminate . . . and conversely, a red one will illuminate if it is rejected, along with the code identifying the error, as previously discussed."

Then he handed Schatten a small manual that outlined the entire process and included a list of codes and the meaning of each. "This book contains everything you'll need to work the system. Guard it with your life and always keep it with you. I think that you can assume that Karamov has the same text in his possession.

"If you receive a red light, the computer will print out one or possibly a series of codes explaining where the errors lie. It's up to you to review the story, correct the errors, and resubmit it. Remember that you have one week to pull this off. It begins at midnight on the day when you receive the entire manuscript."

"Please go over what you said concerning the classified system that I will be allowed to use," said Schatten.

"To ensure that security is not an issue, do not remain in the database system for a period longer than one, I repeat, *one* hour at a time. Even this portal is not flawless. The security system will recognize an anomaly such as this eventually unless the access is limited to one-hour segments. You must terminate after this time interval, and you cannot print out anything at any time while inside it. Nor can you get back in the system for an hour after you log off. This is extremely important. You can only make notes, and that's all. This is key, do you understand? Is everything clear?"

"He is cleverly using the computer to store his submittal piecemeal until he can present the missing sections that will put the entire plot in motion. It's rather like creating a picture puzzle. He has many of the elements in place but has yet to assemble it."

Chelston broke down the entirety of the Russian's plan thus submitted, showing him the text that his group had recorded.

He cautioned that some of the storyline might be a ruse and that only after midnight on the date, when everything was submitted, would the total true story unfold. Once this seven-day period expired, the plot could never again be offered. This was a safeguard built into the system.

"The bottom line is that your mission is to pattern your countermoves in sync with his. Try and put your mind in his, think like him. Know the man, understand his thinking process, and then defeat him using his own techniques."

Schatten began to smirk.

"You find this amusing, Mr. Schatten?"

"Who wouldn't? A week ago I was suffering from writer's block, now I'm the world's only hope."

"But think of it, Michael . . . if by some quirk of chance, he made his story into reality but you alone were the one to defeat him, wouldn't that at least provide you the confidence that you could write with the best?"

Schatten smiled, feeling like David about to take on Goliath. "How can you trust a guy like me with no security clearance of any kind? I bet your superiors would frown on that."

"It's too late in the game to worry about that. Besides, I have full authority to get the job done in a crisis such as this. Security is a minor issue now, my boy. But rest assured, we did check you out in depth before we tried to recruit you."

"What are you saying? You were following me?"

"Let's just say we know your financial situation and that we can solve it."

He handed Schatten a small leather briefcase. "Here's one hundred thousand to get you started, as a measure of good faith; yours to keep, tax free, regardless. That should defer the cost of putting that prized best seller of yours on the back burner for now."

"It will take more than that to solve my finances," replied Schatten.

"Okay, how much?"

"Ugh, I don't know . . . half a million," he blurted without thinking, hands flailing.

"Done!" replied Chelston. "Another five hundred thousand deposited in a Swiss account when you successfully finish the mission."

"Oh come on. Are you serious? You can't really expect me to believe that."

"I have the authority, make no mistake about that. It will be yours, tax free, in an account that only you and I will know exists."

"How'd you know about my book, anyway?" asked Schatten.

"Oh, we make it our business to know."

"Another question," said Schatten.

"Anything dear boy, what is it?"

"Why not just unplug the SAM?"

"Well that is the obvious question, isn't it? The truth is that the SAM has its own funding line and is classified above top secret. It has its own repair technicians, electrical, and software engineers as well as a security force. It is woven so deeply in the military and intelligence fabric that it remains in operation twenty-four hours a day. It monitors threats in all forms and tracks anyone they see fit to surveil. It is a 'black project' that answers to only a select few military types. Its security force keeps their vigil day and night and are mandated to guard it with their lives if necessary. No one quite knows what it does, but there is an unlimited budget to do it. It is buried deep underground in an unknown location. Powered by its own electrical grid, it's rumored that it controls the entire defensive missile system worldwide and monitors threats both terrestrial and extraterrestrial."

"Okay, why not power down your Tesla transmitter?"

"It too has national security implications. Even I don't know what it can do. It's undergone several modifications. It's rumored that it has the power to stop hurricanes and tornados or use them as weapons. It can also shoot down missiles. It never sleeps and is under constant guard along with the SAM."

Schatten exhaled and shook his head as the professor escorted him from the house.

"Michael, you can do this, and call me when you have any issues."

"Thanks," he uttered before proceeding the six blocks to his car, carefully balancing the box the professor had given him, while holding the briefcase. It wasn't heavy, but his arms still ached after reaching his car. He carefully laid the box on the ground and fumbled for his keys before opening the trunk and placing everything inside. He checked his watch; he knew that he must proceed back to his beach house at all speed to begin reading what was available from the noted author. Would his metal hold or would the pressure be too much? He was about to undertake the adventure of a lifetime. If he was the victor, he would save humanity. If not . . . the alternative was too repulsive to envision. But in either case, would anyone ever know?

"Maybe it would make an interesting novel," he mused as he drove back to face his destiny.

1
THE FACE OF THE ENEMY

§CHATTEN WENT DIRECTLY TO THE oceanfront cottage and removed the box from his trunk. He installed the printer and computer easily with the instructions provided. It interfaced seamlessly with the typewriter, using an adapter unlike any he had ever seen.

He tested the computer and printer to assure that they were fully operational. Then he practiced on the typewriter to see if the computer would pick up the entry . . . and it did. His first order of business was to read through the instruction manual that came with his typewriter. It was a training guide that explained every detail and how the overall system functioned. Everything was based upon the one-week cycle, from a plot's inception to its transition into reality. This would also afford him with the opportunity to gain some perspective into what Karamov used to broaden his understanding of the system.

Next, he began reading the text that Chelston had provided him to get a feel as to what he could expect. His initial assessment was that the text was disjointed, as though the man was describing events and places that were seemingly unrelated. Hour after hour, he browsed through the pages and tried to make sense of it. Apparently, there were other portions of the work that preceded this body of work, which gave Chelston's group further insight into the author's intentions.

He wasn't concerned, as he would be privy to everything inside the Karamov file on the hard drive. But as he read further, it was as though the author was sketching out the framework of a plot without revealing precise details.

By the time he read through the entire offering, it was very late on the first day. He used the time allotted to conduct research regarding the nations involved. Russia was prominent, with Iran, China, Syria, and the US. He had a rough picture of the state of the countries about to be immersed in the plot and the social chaos in the regions surrounding the former Soviet Union.

Schatten plugged in the modem that Chelston had given him, and it provided the ability to search the web. Schatten used it to gain a deeper understanding of the regions mentioned in the Karamov file.

He reread everything, marking areas that looked more significant than others and scribbling notes in the margins of his printouts and the electronic pages. Schatten paid special attention to character names and functions. Then, new text began to arrive daily, and before he knew it, two days had passed. He still hadn't entered the classified database but had it high on his agenda for the coming week.

Schatten spent a good part of his time transferring his novel from hardcopy to his laptop.

He was getting low on supplies, and so his priority was to venture into town to stock up on food as a precursor to the upcoming literary war. When he returned, he hung a calendar on the wall of the living room and circled June 24. This was the day that he had envisioned for the arrival of the entire, final version of the text, signaling the beginning of hostilities. He had no desire to be rushed and was satisfied that he would be prepared when the time came. Having stocked the refrigerator, freezer, and the kitchen shelves with food, he made a sandwich and consumed it at the table, while he read the latest offering from the printer. He walked outside to the porch and sat in a lawn chair basking in the sun, where he continued to pour over the many pages of new text.

Schatten glanced at his watch; it was nearly six o'clock in the evening. He went inside, removed a frozen dinner from the freezer, and inserted it into the microwave. Then he went for a short swim. He walked down the beach to find a spot where the water depth was up to his waist. He crouched down and was immediately hit by a succession of large waves.

He recalled one of the driving events in his life that compelled him to take up the gauntlet that Chelston had thrown down. In junior college, Schatten had used his entire Christmas vacation to write what he considered a masterful term paper. It was all that stood between him and an F in an English composition course. His back was against the wall; he had to get an A to salvage a C out of the class.

The subject was Evolution vs. the Bible, and Schatten argued that the theory of evolution and the concept of creation were synonymous. The topic was to be researched and the credits listed in a bibliography, but Schatten's treatise was purely drawn from his imagination. The only references he employed were used to ensure that he properly spelled the names of the various prehistoric creatures featured in the work and give the appearance that he had actually used source material.

After winter break, rife with anticipation and foreboding, he sat on the edge of his seat in the classroom as the instructor slowly made his way to the front of the room to sit on the edge of his desk. Holding the term papers in his left hand, he admonished each student to come to the front and receive their grade for this assignment as well as their final grade, marked on the front sheet. But before he announced the name of each writer, he shared his feelings about every composition.

"This work was extremely well conceived and written and given an A+."

Schatten was poised to rise and retrieve his work, but to his chagrin heard, "Mr. Thomas Smith, excellent work."

Smith rose, walked to the teacher's desk, and received his paper and walked out grinning.

"This next work was also well prepared and thought out. Ms. Albert, come get your A."

This nauseating spectacle repeated itself through the As, Bs, Cs, Ds and finally . . .

"This last paper was obviously copied with no thought whatsoever," said the instructor.

Schatten leaped to his feet. "Is that mine?"

"Yes, it is Mr. Schatten."

Schatten walked briskly up to the man and snatched the ten-page submission from his grip. "You might as well give me my F now."

"Oh, it's already been done."

Schatten left the building, seething, and walked around the block. Somehow he had to make this right. After pounding the pavement for a half an hour and regaining control, he went to the dean. Schatten explained his situation and pleaded his case. The dean set up a meeting the next day between the teacher and Schatten. It was agreed that Schatten would be allowed to compose a work in one hour in the teacher's office to demonstrate that the work was his and not plagiarized.

The following day, Schatten reported to Atwell's office at precisely at 9 a.m. where he was given five sheets of paper and told to compose an abbreviated version of the term paper. He put everything he had into it. The next day, Schatten reported to the dean's office where he was informed that he had earned a C out of the course.

He never forgot that battle. A case where the gauntlet had been thrown down and he had accepted the challenge. And now, he found himself in a similar situation, ready to prove himself once more.

Returning to his house, he consumed his meal in rapid order along with a glass of cranberry juice. Realizing he was as ready as he'd ever be, he turned on the television and relaxed on the couch. Now all he could do was wait. His eyes became heavy, and soon he fell asleep. He woke briefly at 11:45 p.m. and noted that the printer still hadn't received anything further and wondered briefly when he would see the next offering before he started to doze off once more.

He didn't have to wait long. Precisely at the stroke of midnight, his printer furiously consumed paper, as reams of prose burst forth. He stirred momentarily, listening to see when the flurry of activity would stop, but it didn't.

Startled, he leaped to his feet and began pulling off the pages to clear a path for the next sheets and to read over the gist of each offering. Trying to clear his head, he was suddenly hit with the realization that D-Day was here.

"It can't be, it's too soon." he mumbled, as the printer threw out pages, unabated.

He cleared off a section of the living room coffee table and began to pile the myriad of text upon it. Schatten had purchased a large box of paper along with the groceries and soon had to cut through the two plastic bands to remove the lid. He tore open a block of paper and reloaded the printer. It was spewing pages almost as fast as he could remove them; certainly faster than he could read them. He began to stack the pages in piles of fifty. Not knowing when the flow would stop, he began to quickly scan the first pages while waiting for the printer to amass the latest twenty or so. Then he scooped them up and placed them on the table with the rest of the sheets. He was beginning to feel like the little wizard in the sorcerer's apprentice trying to stem the flow of water from the well and the magic brooms' buckets. In this case, it was paper from the printer. The sound of each printed page was grinding on his nerves and ears.

The title was *Armageddon Revisited*. Detailed and extremely descriptive, it dealt with several key characters.

The primary antagonist was Ernst von Weir, described as an Austrian and a confirmed Nazi.

He circled the character's name and put a checkmark by the page number. His anti-Semitism was only matched by his loathing of Arabs, and he considered himself a product of the Aryan aristocracy.

His father, now deceased, was a wealthy businessman tied to the automotive industry. Von Weir's grandfather had been a major player in wartime munitions and part of Hitler's inner circle.

His grandmother was an Austrian countess, but her liberal views on the plight of the Jews and the Holocaust was a constant source of embarrassment to his grandfather during the war. After Germany's defeat, he tried distancing himself from any postwar retribution by hiding behind his wife's humanitarian beliefs.

Von Weir secretly embraced his father's views of Germany ruling the world, both economically and militarily, harboring a great hatred for Bolshevism.

There was only one person that von Weir did trust. His only confidante was a former colleague in the Special Forces who was also a writer and his biographer. It would be this individual who would document von Weir's many victories and his ascension to unequivocal power. That man was Ian Androkov, who served as von Weir's alter ego. Androkov kept a low profile, was very intelligent and rather unpretentious. Like von Weir, he was also mysterious.

The physical description of Androkov was nothing less than a self-portrait of Karamov, down to the small scars on his left wrist, which Chelston had clearly established for Schatten's benefit, even presenting him with pictures of the writer.

Having established the core about which all the evil revolved, Karamov's writings delved into the others that made up the treacherous alliance. Schatten continued to pour over the text, but the actual plot was obscure as the cavalcade of characters continued. So he kept searching for something tangible that he could lock onto as a base. But he thought that it was important to know the nature of the characters involved to see the types of personalities with which he was contending and therefore learn the substance of the play from its players.

He sifted through dozens more pages but saw nothing of substance and thought that all the icons of the plot had appeared. When by shear happenstance, he started reading another section, and he realized that he was mistaken.

The rest of the ensemble was composed of role players emanating from diverse regions, stretching from the Ukraine to Istanbul, where political refugees, traitors, cutthroats, assassins, religious zealots, and soldiers of fortune rubbed shoulders in a montage of ideologies and temperaments.

The common goals were power, greed, and vengeance. Schatten noted that the missing element in all cases was that of conscience. It was this volatile mix that von Weir would mold into a fighting force to do his sinister bidding. All the conspirators would be handsomely compensated to recreate the world order in their own respective images.

It was clear that unscrupulous hordes were gathering, but the text that followed added nothing to clarify the overall design of the master plan. Instead, the next litany of pages dealt with even more characters, describing each and his role and skill set in vivid detail.

But as Schatten waded through the dozens of soldiers, sailors, and technicians sculpted by the author's pen, he was led to the inescapable fact that high levels of technology were required for this author's plan to work, along with highly trained military personnel. It was as though Karamov was positioning figures on a number of chessboards, taking great pains to identify each, and making sure that every player fit neatly onto the stage where the drama would play out. Schatten continued to monitor the printer and wondered if it would ever end.

He kept a watchful eye on the clock to see how long the device had been printing. The only time that it halted was when the paper would run out. He kept his vigil, restocking the tray with fresh paper as though he were feeding a dragon with a voracious appetite. His emotions ran the gambit between anger and fear as the sound of the printer never wavered in its output.

As the minute hand hit 3:55 a.m., the printer fell silent. He looked at the last sheet to be printed and saw the number 550 at the bottom of the page with no clear indication that this was the end.

"He's writing *War and Peace!*" Schatten shouted, as he angrily launched his pencil across the room, head and shoulders slumping from exhaustion while still scanning through the entire offering. The incessant sound of the printer was becoming like fingernails on a chalkboard.

Then he stopped his tirade and uttered, "Easy boy, it's only just begun."

Schatten continued to read on as the sun's light began to creep into the room. He had been going for four hours when he decided to rest. Grateful that no more installments were forthcoming and that he might have found the end to the trail, he laid on the couch and drifted off.

8
THE MEETING OF THE MINDS

SCHATTEN AWOKE TO SILENCE. HE ROSE immediately from the couch and looked at the printer resting on the center of the living room table. There he saw the paper jam symbol.

"Are you kiddin' me?" he snapped.

Schatten immediately opened the printer doors, searching for a crumpled-up sheet. He found it after several minutes and pulled out the culprit. The error code vanished when he closed all the doors. He loaded twenty sheets to hear the printer spewing sheet after sheet; it was alive once more. Schatten had been asleep for five hours. He immediately went about the task of assembling the pages and organizing them. Still disoriented, he suddenly remembered that page number 550 was the last sheet he had read before he dozed off.

He retrieved his pencil he had launched into the other room and began to sort the sheets into groups once more as his stomach growled. Schatten knew that he had to keep up his strength for the marathon to come. He wanted to go into town and have a huge breakfast, but he did not want to leave the manuscript and waste any more time. Instead, he settled for cereal and juice, hoping it would sustain him long into the afternoon.

Schatten feverishly began to sift through the mountain of pages. He removed a pen from a box laying alongside the printer and began to make notes on every sheet that contained a reference to any character. Then he began to think up categories such as sailors, soldiers, and terrorists that might help him organize the flow of paper that seemed to be going on forever. He began to scribble the categories on the backs of some of the used paper.

Then he laid the sheets in front of each pile to identify the category, starting with main characters, then he made subgroups for lesser types by nationality.

Schatten realized that the printer could not print at this level for long without changing ink cartridges. He wondered whether the box of paper he had previously purchased would be enough to support the effort; if this was a sample of how much text he could expect on a daily basis. Then he realized that Chelston had told him that all the text would be sent at the same time.

The printer continued to turn out sheet after sheet until finally, some five hours later, it stopped. He nervously looked at the last page and saw the word "END" at the bottom of page 1201. He smirked, took in a deep breath, puffed up his cheeks, and exhaled slowly. Then he savored the silence.

Revisionist Future

Please let this be all of it, he thought.

Now that he knew the extent of Karamov's submission, he began in earnest to finish the organization of the full text and find the plot. He continued to consolidate the sheets by page number and characters. There was no table of contents, nor were there any chapter titles, only the page numbers.

The professor was right, thought Schatten. This is not your standard manuscript.

Schatten began to highlight characters with colored markers. Green was for the primary leaders, blue for their subordinates, and yellow for the grunts. He scribbled notes in the margins of various pages for later reference. It was soon obvious that there were too many characters to color code. He used a notebook to record his comments. As he did so, he noticed some common threads.

Schatten also used the computer to generate a spreadsheet so he could track characters, their functions, and how much each influenced the storyline. As his mind began to clear, he realized that he was going in too many directions.

He picked up a sheet of paper and with a black marker, printed in large letters,

FIND THE PLOT!

Then he placed it in the center of the table.

What was it? How does one take over the world without a massive army?

He tracked events in the story, noting their connection to other parts of the story. As he scanned his way through the mountain of text, the foundation of the diabolical plot began to manifest itself.

"Ah, here we go," said Schatten feeling like Sherlock Holmes finally finding the details of the mystery.

It began to unfold in a meeting held secretly in a spacious, long-abandoned warehouse in the outskirts of Baku, Azerbaijan.

Von Weir had paid off all the local officials to ensure his privacy. There, he addressed the entire villainous contingent of hand-picked conspirators. They had gathered to hear the insidious plans to topple the established halls of power and replace order with anarchy. Offering a modest but diverse spread, including caviar—he excluded alcohol to placate the Islamic faction and to be assured that his message would be received by clear heads—von Weir was careful to make each individual feel important and completely at ease. He created an atmosphere in which each sect felt as though they were the primary beneficiaries of the scheme and the mainstays of the entire operation.

The mastermind remained hidden before mingling unnoticed with the crowd, wearing a drab, hooded sweatsuit. He wanted to feel the pulse of the contingent and hear the commentary. Each man was handed a series of instructions to follow once they arrived. Every individual's name was on the sheets further adding to the illusion of his importance. Von Weir's personal guard roamed all sectors of the gathering to insure orderly behavior. They were also clad in drab sweatsuits as not to alarm any of this unsavory group. When he was ready to begin, the maestro stealthily moved behind the stage and slipped into a business suit. He entered the dark, elevated stage unseen and sat in a padded chair just behind the podium. Once he perceived that all were settling, he slowly rose to his feet.

As everyone began to take their seats, he ordered the lights to be dimmed. Von Weir walked over to a light switch just to the left of the white wall behind him that served as the backdrop.

He flicked the switch, and a beam focused on the center of the stage. Then he walked back to the lectern, immersed himself in the spotlight, and adjusted the microphone. Von Weir looked down upon the masses from above. From his position behind the dark oak podium, overlooking the expansive room, he surveyed all the activity before him.

"Would everyone please be seated, and may I have your attention."

Most took paper plates and filled them with varieties of food and retrieved drinks laid out on rows of tables that lined the room before positioning themselves on the padded folding chairs provided. With remote control in hand, von Weir activated a computer containing slides of his presentation.

Like an entrepreneur adeptly selling his concepts to clientele, von Weir hawked his plan to usurp the power of the world's key players and channel it into his own hands. The long shadow of the man and the podium presented a surreal vision and, coupled with the penetrating sound system, reeked of power.

"Gentlemen, I give you the new world order!" yelled von Weir, right fist clenched and raised, watching the screen as it showed every face assembled.

He went down the entire group, one by one, stating the role and the importance of each in the master plan. Von Weir was careful to treat each individual as though they were indispensable.

"I've spoken to every person in this room, so there is no need for introductions. You were handpicked to be part of this operation. What I'm offering each of you is the chance to shape the world into what you envision it to be. I think you all know why you're here, but just to refresh your memories, I mean to rid the world of the status quo, the old regimes that shackle all of us. I mean to clear the air of the stench of Zionist thinking, US influence, and all those that currently sit on the seats of power!"

This was met with thunderous applause and screaming. After a moment, von Weir asked for calm, and the men quickly became silent.

"Gentleman, in order to play with the big boys, one requires big toys. I propose to obtain the bargaining chips to play in such a game. I am talking about high-tech weaponry with nuclear capability, both land- and sea-based."

This caused an immediate rumble through the contingent.

"Silence if you please, gentlemen. Let us begin with aerial and satellite photos of our quarry."

Using his laser pointer, he drew everyone's attention to the screen. Von Weir did not immediately identify the actual targets shown to the assembly, but he did divulge what the plot involved.

"I mean to pirate a Soviet Typhoon-class ballistic missile submarine while taking a Russian

ICBM complex," he said calmly, as if it were a walk in the park.

"Wow, there it is, but how do you expect to pull this off?" muttered Schatten.

These chief objectives offered the blueprint of the entire plot that Karamov had only alluded to in his preliminary discussions with each of them. He was all business and kept the levity to a minimum. This invoked an immediate buzz, along with jeers, shouts, and conversation as the reaction swept through the gathering as each man provided a commentary to those seated around them.

"Order, gentlemen, order!" von Weir bellowed, forcible but controlled to ensure his dominance.

Both his positioning above the gathering and his quick response to anything that threatened to detract from his presentation was a preplanned demonstration of his authority. Von Weir would now establish his prowess as the leader to the entire assembly. Through his powerful voice, body language, and command of numerous languages, he impressed the gathering, reminding them who was in charge. Presenting a minimum of generalities, he concentrated on small details that, when assembled, created a plan so audacious that it shocked everyone of the entire criminal group in attendance. This was significant since every man in the room had a different modus operandi. Von Weir's comprehensive approach to a seemingly impossible concept soon planted the seeds of feasibility into every mind.

The look of disbelief on numerous faces was displaced with smiles as von Weir presented his devious scheme, which appealed to even the audience's most ardent skeptics. He insisted that surprise and timing were paramount to this venture's success; that the danger was offset by scrupulous attention to detail and planning. But he added that the limitless rewards outweighed any hazard.

Then he abruptly terminated the slide presentation and gave instructions for the entire contingent to meet at a secret training facility near the city of Makhachkala in the Republic of Dagestan by the Caspian Sea.

Its remoteness made it a perfect training area, and its diverse population would ensure that the group would blend into the environment.

He had purchased an abandoned farm containing the remains of a former Soviet army training facility. The area was far enough from the local populous not to raise suspicion and to assure that any explosions or gunfire associated with the training would go unnoticed. The leaders of the community welcomed the revenue, and the land had long since been abandoned when it was learned that mines had been planted by the previous tenants and never removed. Von Weir was shrewd enough to recognize this and told representatives of the local community that this was part of the reason they had come; to restore the safety of the land once they completed their activities. He claimed that some ordinance would be employed to detonate the mines, which provided the perfect smoke screen for their mission.

As the meeting disbanded, each member of the sinister alliance was given a map to the training facility and told when to reconvene.

The meeting successfully conducted, all agreed to report for the next stage of the plan without incident. But von Weir had no illusions about this assembly of cutthroats. He knew that the extremists could perform as a team until such time as each of them had achieved their personal objectives. Then it was merely a question of time before one or all would turn on any other member to attain more. He concocted a scheme to limit this possibility by secretly negotiating with each man. He offered every individual a handsome sum up front, as a down payment to the final king's ransom. But the price was absolute loyalty, secrecy, and the commitment to spy on the other members. Each was made graphically aware that any breach to this contract would be regarded as treason with total forfeiture of shares, followed by a swift death. He reasoned that all could respect the ironclad rules if the laws were applied unilaterally and fairly without exception.

Von Weir also promised unique things to each and wove a mosaic so intricate that no one, save the man himself, knew the outline of the entire web of deceit. He offered each conspirator a bonus to sell out any other member if caught in a plot to undermine his authority. Von Weir also stated to the group that in addition, any act of sedition could mean the difference between failure and success and the punishment was too gruesome to contemplate. The only way to ensure the success of the project would be for them to police themselves to remove any malefactor.

Any man unwilling to fully cooperate would be ostracized, replaced, and eliminated with extreme prejudice. But if such an event should occur, those remaining would then divide the spoils of the guilty party, with the lion's share going to that individual who turned in the culprit. Von Weir would serve as the arbiter and judge, but the group would vote on the evidence compiled.

But if the party was indispensable, von Weir knew that he could always conjure up evidence to refute the accusations to reinstate the accused until he accomplished the mission. But this would merely be a stay of execution.

He broke the entire assembly into six groups. The Islamic contingent—mostly from Iraq, Syria, Pakistan, and Afghanistan—was led by Mohammad Izobyer and formed two of the six; the Russian naval personnel, anchored by Alexander Setski, comprised the third; the Russian Special Forces, under Ivan Pushlin, a fourth group; the fifth and sixth divisions were composed of a mix of various extremists and additional Russian factions who would serve as backup, mobile reserves, and immediate replacements also under Pushlin and Izobyer.

Over a series of three days, von Weir talked with each group, going over every detail. He established the leaders and ensured that each group was a cohesive unit.

Each team would have a precise goal, but no one, save those inside that group, would know of its activities. All they were told was that on a precise date, they would be in position to negotiate with the entire world on their terms.

The groups led by Pushlin and Izobyer practiced for two weeks in the abandoned farm facility, simulating the missile complex.

Mohammad Izobyer came from a royal family in Syria. He was schooled in the United States and France and began his college career studying medicine before changing his major and receiving a degree as a civil engineer.

But his disillusion with the West and his following of Islamic extremism led him to von Weir's door.

Von Weir implanted and cultivated the vision of the restoration of the Assyrian or Persian Empires with the exploits of Izobyer occupying the same place in history with other legends of past glories reserved for the likes of Sennacherib, Ashurbanipal, and other great conquerors. Von Weir's cunning was particularly evident in this relationship, as he used his anti-Semitic bias to foster the goals of Izobyer and bolster his ego while viewing him and his countrymen as vermin.

Deceit was a quality upon which von Weir prided himself and summarized by the words he had once confided to Androkov, "Be all things to all people as it fits your objectives, but respect and trust no one."

They drilled continuously, emulating the setting of explosives to breach the inside escape hatch before running through the tunnels, rooms, and hallways to capture the missile control room in smoked-filled conditions. Tear gas was substituted for the actual toxin to be deployed that would kill the inhabitants inside the complex. Then their Russian ex-Special Forces, led by Ivan Pushlin, would storm the facility as Izobyer's mercenaries stood guard outside to defend against a counterattack and act as backup. Pushlin would be in charge and determine when they were ready. Only Setski's group would not engage in this exercise.

Pushlin was a former officer in the Soviet army special forces. Suddenly unemployed once the Cold War world order had crumbled, Pushlin turned to the Russian underworld to take advantage of the new capitalistic system. He became no more than a thug, doing the bidding of his superiors in the Russian mafia.

Von Weir offered that in truth, America was exploiting his people to foster the designs of Israel and continue their territorial expansion and colonialism. This also provided a basis upon which to build the support for the Arab cause and identify the common enemy.

The last group with which von Weir convened was Alexander Setski's. From the moment the two entered the room, the air was permeated by resentment and distrust, for neither shared the same views on the mission.

Setski started the meeting by demanding a force twice what von Weir had envisioned. Von Weir was outraged at the ferocity of Setski's verbal attack, but he was smart enough to understand the pivotal role that the naval man played. Von Weir calmly explained that if the full complement took charge of the craft, it might raise suspicions from all quarters. But a boat manned by only a skeleton crew conducting sea trials on a secret defensive device might very well pass scrutiny for a period long enough to hijack their prize.

"Okay, how do you pirate a Soviet nuclear submarine, Karamov?" mumbled Schatten, scribbling notes in the column of the page he had just read.

Schatten reasoned that he must discern quickly what the complement of a typical Soviet underwater craft was and what skills were required to operate such a vessel. He then would get into the intricacies of the boat's weaknesses and all its associated systems and armament as soon as he could determine the exact type of craft being discussed.

The computer had become silent for some time, but Schatten kept his ear tuned for any additional outpouring of pages while his eyes continuously scanned through the text. After a few hours of this, he decided to make himself a sandwich and rest his eyes. Upon finishing his meal, he decided to enter the inner sanctum of the classified database to which Chelston had given him access.

9
THE SUBMARINERS

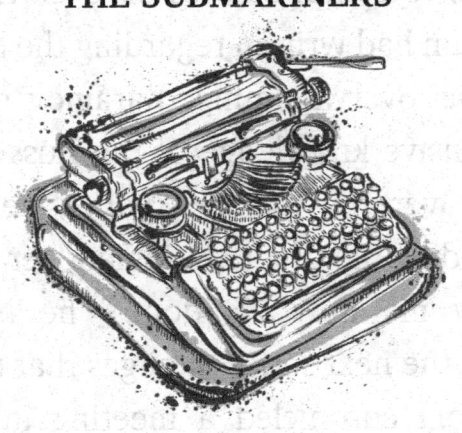

S CHATTEN WAS NERVOUS AS HE REMOVED the small notebook containing the entry codes from the envelope that Chelston had provided. He took a deep breath and approached the keyboard. He glanced over the myriad of passwords and instruction steps deftly outlined by the good professor. But then he paused, realizing that he knew virtually nothing on the topic of Russian vessels.

So rather than jump into the database with no sense of direction, he decided to use Karamov's writing as the means to provide an introduction. He began to compile notes on everything that the Russian had written regarding the boat. The detail was overwhelming. Karamov obviously had extensive knowledge of the Russian Navy. Pouring over the mass of paper, he became enthralled by the plot to commandeer the sub.

"Show me how it's done," he muttered, scanning the next series of pages that told him.

The text chronicled a meeting in a small village on the Black Sea between factions of the Russian Army and Navy organized by Alexander Setski, known to all and respected as a no-nonsense leader. Setski was the shrewdest member of the group and a former naval commander, Special Forces operative, and KGB officer. It was he who had ties to all the paramilitary groups inside Russia as well as other parts of the former Soviet Union and to members and former members of the Russian Navy. It would be his men who would provide the skills, expertise, leadership, and highly trained individuals to execute the von Weir vision. Without them, the plan would fail.

Setski understood this all too clearly. Because of this, he was a bane to von Weir. Neither man trusted the other. But their common hatred of the United States formed a strange bond between the two. The Russian was smart and well-educated. He had attended several Russian universities and had a family naval heritage stemming back to the First World War. He was part of the extremists who advocated going to war with the Americans. He even volunteered once to provide the provocation. He was shut out of the new regime when Boris Yeltsin came to power. He was a hard-liner personified and still harbored resentment over the Nazi's ravaging of his country. Von Weir offered that Hitler had made an egregious error in breaking his alliance with the Russians and that the two should have united against the West. Then, von Weir gave his assurance that all would be rectified if Setski would captain his aggressive plan and deal the US its deathblow, along with the traitors in his own country and China. He could then dictate his own foreign policy and rule Russia itself. Von Weir not only offered unlimited power but a lucrative down payment as well.

Setski invited a contingent of the most influential and authoritative figures working inside the Sevastopol naval depot repair complex. The Russian knew precisely how corrupt the group was and brought enough hard cash to open the eyes of the most ardent skeptics.

Part of the massive sum that von Weir provided Setski was to be used to appropriate storage and overhaul facilities to modify a single vessel with his special equipment. As though he were engaged in the process of locating and buying a used car, Setski began negotiations to "borrow," as he put it, a Typhoon-class Russian submarine with full nuclear missile launch capability.

This required that an entire network chain of specialists be enlisted, bribed, and deceived including weapons experts, political officials, guards, logisticians, security personnel, naval officials, inspectors, and repair specialists. None of these people were told the nature of the activity that required such an acquisition, only that it was highly classified. All of them had the impression that Setski was still employed by the Navy. His standing as an icon within the ranks of the submariner community legitimized the scheme in everyone's mind.

What simplified his task immensely was the simple fact that the Soviet Navy had been in a state of disarray for some time. Funding had been drastically cut to such an extent that many of the ships were not seaworthy. Thus, any source that offered to pay for a complete overhaul of a vessel would have the attention of the entire shipyard. The offer was simple but effective; he would pay for the complete renovation of the ship if he could use it for his test trials. Then the naval unit to which it was assigned would be presented with a fully operational vessel, which in the standards of the day, was a luxury. Only the newest vessels warranted the funds from on high to complete extensive repairs or perform scheduled overhauls and calibrate complex system arrays. The older models were left to be cannibalized or sailed only partially operational in a reserve capacity. The latter was important, for if a ship remained out of service too long, it would be written off and never supported monetarily. If Setski refrained from trying to commandeer a front-line vessel, his odds of success were good . . . as long as his security smoke screen and his cash flow held.

His hand-picked contingency that accompanied him, including known political officers, offered all the earmarks of a top secret, clandestine project for which the Soviets had been famous over the years. Setski started slowly, enlisting those that owed him favors within the intelligence community and the Navy. He confided, in vague generalities, of a plan to install an experimental device aboard a test vessel. The modification offered it the ability to successfully breech any anti-submarine defense by emulating the signature of any known ship. Due to the stealthiness of all modern underwater craft, the only method to track any of these craft was to monitor the sounds created by the machinery that drove the ship. Each vessel had its own unique signature, and therefore, each could be cataloged inside the memory of a computer which could match the sound signature to the actual vessel once a ship's sensor array recorded its presence.

Von Weir discovered a device that promised to change the sound signature of any submarine to emulate that of any desired vessel. Thus, a Russian sub could masquerade as a US sub or any nationality by simply employing the equipment. He backed the project and threw tons of capital at it to refine the concept and correct the glaring weaknesses. The system that emerged was state-of-the-art, and most importantly, it delivered the desired results or so von Weir led everyone to believe. It was this device that Setski would offer the Russians as the lure to allow him access to a submarine for its installation and test. It was a purely defensive system, and so no weaponry would be added that required more scrutiny.

After Setski sold the merits of such a device to his Russian comrades, showing them how it would give them a major advantage over the West, it was simple for all to understand that a level of heightened security must be adopted. Everything was to be accomplished through top secret channels as a black or covert program. It was stressed that only a select few could participate in this venture and that it must be kept from the prying eyes of foreign security services. Setski strengthened the plausibility of the scheme by offering that if the experiment was conducted through normal channels, not only would security be an issue but costs would be prohibitive. He argued that the only way to conduct such a mission in the present economy was to employ a minimum workforce and only use the cream of the crop in all aspects, which stroked the egos of everyone involved. The incentive would be to institute an accelerated pay scale to all, which carried the expectation of an accelerated, round-the-clock schedule.

Setski would first enlist the aid of those individuals who had previously worked on the overhaul of a large vessel with missile launch capability. A ship would be selected which was in the system scheduled for overhaul but delayed by the normal bureaucracy.

An abbreviated timetable would be established to prepare the ship, far ahead of its scheduled return to service. This would give him a fully operational weapons platform that by all actual paperwork should still be in dry-dock. The top secret moniker would allow the stealth device to be fitted to the drive system but not be reflected in the documentation via the paid off inspectors.

Large sums of money were distributed as Setski enlisted the core individuals capable of locating a suitable ship that would serve as the basic platform for the terrorists before implementing the installation of the cloaking device. Only a select few would know of the actual cover story that Setski was disseminating. Those providing the labor would only know that they were being highly compensated to participate in a program of national security, which they were mandated not to discuss.

Setski met individually with each person associated with the venture. In this way, he had a feel for everyone involved. He instilled the illusion of national pride into each participant and established the false impression that the exercise was legitimate and sanctioned by the Kremlin.

The speech he gave to all involved would seal the air of secrecy. "There are those within the government who don't want this project to succeed for obvious reasons. They think that it would put us in a bad light with the Americans."

These lines alone would normally have been enough to convince any Russian to enlist, but Setski would add even more during each interview. There, he would let each potential recruit know that they had been handpicked because of their political views and work record. His contacts in the FSB had given him the dossiers on everyone being enlisted so that Setski knew each individual's party leaning prior to the interview.

It was important to bribe everyone, from the lowest technician to the highest inspector. Intelligence officers would monitor the conversations of the workers to ensure that nothing was being divulged outside the facility. Aside from the installation of the device, the entire boat had to be overhauled and brought up to full operational capability. This required technical experts from all ends of the spectrum; encompassing electronics, sonar, weapons, hydraulics, pneumatics, mechanics, and those trained on nuclear reactors. Trying to sift through this vast array of specialists to find not only those that were qualified but those that would cooperate willingly was daunting. But Setski was as relentless in this activity as he was as a former ship's captain. His diligence and scrupulous devotion to detail above all else made the plan work.

Von Weir counted upon such traits, giving Setski complete charge of this phase of the operation. He could always reel him in if need be.

Once the craft was selected and the facility identified, Setski sealed off the area. No one would question such a move since the normal bureaucracy made it impossible for anyone to really know what went on inside such facilities.

Setski grasped that his increased level of security would certainly not be looked upon with suspicion. Instead, everyone embraced the perspective that something must have occurred to cause this heightened added secrecy to be imposed. Questioning the decision might only lead to possible political involvement, which everyone avoided at all costs. In short, Setski skillfully manipulated the system to serve his goals.

With the boat and overhaul facility identified, Setski went to the most crucial and dangerous part of his mission. First, he offered a king's ransom for the borrowing (liberation) of a complement of missiles with their nuclear warheads and torpedoes from several dry-docked submarines. Logisticians would also be enlisted to obtain these items by ensuring that all the hardware was aptly misplaced within the system. Then, the inventories would be altered to place these items in either retired or overhaul status. This created a series of questions from both the security types and the military. He stressed that he needed the missiles for his sea trials to simulate the actual reaction of the entire ship to the operation of the cloaking device. They had to ensure that none of the launch capabilities were compromised and no unnecessary vibrations, or electrical overloading, occurred as a result of the installation of the experimental equipment. They also had to maintain the proper weight and balance. They would merely use the weapons for several days before returning them, rectifying the inventories while all involved received ridiculous compensation and accolades. It was the new business approach at work to streamline the system and overcome the bureaucracy.

Every individual working on the ship was paid in segments. This was to ensure that all would keep working with an incentive to do the job properly. In addition, all were promised a bonus if the work was completed earlier than scheduled. Everyone knew not to discuss the amount of payment with anyone within the ranks. Any indication of discontent with the amount of cash received would not be tolerated and would be dealt with immediately. Setski's no-nonsense approach would serve notice that he meant business. He constantly inspected the work, and all felt his presence.

Women were hired for added security and were lucratively compensated for any information divulged by anyone associated with the project. It was their mission to be stationed strategically at the local bars to solicit conversations with the crews involved with the work. Any confidential information reported would immediately be transmitted to Setski's security force and the individual reprimanded. This, along with listening devices planted in homes, around the ship, and in break areas and vehicles, instilled fear into everyone. Speculations ran wild as to who was informing on whom or how the security force was gathering the information as paranoia reigned.

It was like old times, and many welcomed it. Bribing the inspectors ensured that all the records were falsified to reflect that the ship was completely overhauled to all standard specifications. No mention of the stealth device, called the Chameleon, was entered anywhere.

Revisionist Future

Setski's crew made periodic appearances to become acutely familiar with every aspect of the ship, especially the new device. Since the ship's complement would be far less than the normal crew, each would be expected to know considerably more in other areas, beyond what would be considered normal in a standard environment. Setski trained them in multiple assignments and even bought the use of a simulator for sustained hands-on training. Their skill levels soon rose, as did their confidence, and an air of invincibility permeated the crew, as they got closer to the day when they would take charge of the vessel.

Guards as well as anyone associated with the overhaul and refitting were never told when the craft was fully operational. This meant that when the boat was being stolen by the cutthroats, everyone would be told that the ship was to undergo a short series of sea trials with a skeleton crew. Those that did know of the secret device being tested would feel a sense of national pride that they were involved in a black project to vault the Russian navy to a new level of sophistication. While the funds flowed, anyone and their signature could be bought for the right price. But no one understood the gravity of the ominous plot they were fostering. Had they known the men involved were outside Mother Russia and that they were plunging into nuclear war, none would have participated.

Setski convinced everyone that the cash being liberally distributed was government money and not to be reported, due to the classified nature. It was again passed off as a new way of doing business, to cut red tape for highly-sensitive projects. The ruse was that this was as a pilot program to see if this new methodology could be employed across the board and streamline the antiquated system. The concept was so radical that everyone reasoned that surely a man of Setski's stature could not be involved with some sordid operation. Instead, he relied upon their patriotism as well as their greed, but once they had become part of the conspiracy, there was no going back. The thought of making more in a month than most made in ten years was too much of a temptation. Most were told that everyone was doing it and that if anyone failed to participate, one of their co-workers would get their share.

The masking device had been installed over a period of several weeks while the vessel was undergoing normal servicing. Several sensors and vibration damping devices were installed in and around the drive shafts and transmission area. Told that it was an experimental suite of sonar detection avoidance equipment, coded as top secret, inspectors and intelligence officers alike did not dare ask any questions. One high-ranking FSB official, also part of the plot, hovered over the installation, answering all questions and furnishing all the proper paperwork. High-ranking signatures were forged or paid for when necessary.

Since the installation did not involve weaponry or the reactor, it was considered benign by all observers, especially those in the intelligence communities. To make the charade even more palatable, each security officer was told that he alone would be given the inside story on its success or failure after the mission was completed. If successful, each would be prominently mentioned, promoted, and given much of the credit.

As the final hours ticked down, Setski continually poured over every detail of the plan. Sleep eluded him as his thoughts raged. When it was at last time, he took a long shower and gathered his gear for the final visit to the dock and the base. The morning was cold for a spring day, and the air was heavy, laden with moisture. The fog that had rolled into the harbor made visibility poor and added to the ability of the pirates to perform their mission in the poor conditions.

Setski and his first officer, Ivan Rekorski, arrived first, donned in battle gear. Setski saluted the security officials who had amassed about the gangplank. All knew who this legendary man was, but code words were exchanged, and badges shown, nonetheless. The bottom line was that all conditions were go and that there had been no complications. All the missiles were aboard and fully armed along with a full complement of torpedoes.

Revisionist Future

Setski boarded the vessel and saluted the guard on deck. The guards departed as the crew began to file onto the ship. He and his second-in-command welcomed each member and checked each name off the list until the complement was complete. After saluting their commander, each man went below deck to ready the craft for sea.

Setski and his first officer now climbed the steps to the mighty conning tower. There, they looked down on the enormous cylindrical craft and the surrounding area. The smell of salt water, the feel of the conning tower, and the gusting wind on his face exhilarated Setski and negated his lack of sleep. When all were aboard, the captain went below to check on the progress of each seaman. Carrying a clipboard with every system listed along with its assigned crewmember, Setski systematically went through the entire ship. Looking at his watch, he barked at the crew in each corner of the vessel, urging them to move swiftly while stressing attention to detail. When his watch indicated that the time allocated for the ship's preparation had elapsed, he began his final inspection. He started from the forward section of the ship and asked each individual if their task had been completed. If the crewmember did not respond affirmatively, he stayed with the individual until the task was done and his assigned system was fully operational. Employing this technique throughout the vessel, Setski knew precisely what issues he had. Other than minor glitches, which did not have a direct impact on his mission, he was pleased with the efforts of the depot repair team and his crew. His approach to detail gave his recruits a sense that he had complete cognizance of everything. This added to their confidence and desire to emulate the man in the attention given to their assigned tasks. He instilled pride among his men and made each feel important, leaving the impression that if any individual failed to perform his function smartly and correctly, the entire mission could fail.

Satisfied that all checks were complete, the captain picked up the microphone in the control station. There, he set the system to full volume. This, combined with his already booming voice, ensured everyone's attention. "This is the captain," he bellowed, "make all preparations to get underway. Mr. Rekorski ahead one third."

"Aye sir," said his second-in-command. The mooring lines were cast off and the drive system engaged. Setski then took his position in the conning tower. The huge craft slowly moved away from the dock and into the blackness of the channel. Using the intense fog to mask his vessel, Setski remained in the conning tower until the mist began to abate. By then, he was in the open sea, where he ordered the boat to submerge. Once under water, he ordered an extensive check of all systems. As they ventured into deep water, he ordered an exhaustive series of drills following the initial shakedown. They simulated a full missile and torpedo launch, deploying countermeasures, damage assessment, firefighting and contamination containment.

The craft continued its course as Setski's navigator, Andre Cheporich, charted its path precisely against the extensive maps of the ocean floor. Setski knew that he was lucky to have this man as a crew member. Cheporich was one of the finest navigators in the fleet. He had served with Setski for years before a freak accident almost paralyzed him. The Navy forced him into early retirement, leaving him bitter even though he had totally rehabilitated himself. When Setski approached him with this mission, he leaped at the chance to prove the Navy wrong in their assessment of his capabilities.

The ship steered due west from the Black Sea, through the Bosporus into the Sea of Marmara, passed the Dardanelles into the Aegean, and finally, the Mediterranean. Passing through the Straits of Gibraltar, the ship took its position in the North Atlantic where it was poised to strike the United States, the United Kingdom, China, and Russia.

Setski realized that the crew would not consider attacking Mother Russia. Therefore, he alone knew the targets and programmed them himself. It pained him to do so, but he viewed it like cauterizing a wound. It was distasteful but necessary. Besides, Stalin had killed countless thousands of his own people for decades; it was the Russian way.

Yet there was a chance that this action may not be required. If von Weir's other plot—firing the first land-based missile salvo—ignited the powder keg such that all nations would attack the Soviets, it would eliminate his participation in attacking Mother Russia. Hitting the US was another story, as he took distinct pleasure in dealing what he hoped would be the nation's deathblow.

This was the part of the scheme that bothered Schatten the most. Sickened by the plot, he was nonetheless intrigued and obligated to read on.

The ship carried 20 Sturgeon RSM-52/SS-N-20 submarine launched ballistic missiles or SLBM. Each intercontinental ballistic missile carried ten multiple warheads, or MIRVS, with an explosive yield of .1 Megatons. All that was required now was his authorization from von Weir to proceed in initiating the final war. The code word was "Valkyrie" for the actual launch, but to ensure that nothing would go wrong, it would be preceded by two preliminary phrases.

The first was "Sheathe Sword," meaning ready-all-systems, and the second, "Draw Sword," meant to stand by and report to the launch point.

Setski continued his journey, steaming to a position in the mid-Atlantic. Poised to hit both the east coast of the United States and Great Britain, he would now lay in wait for the launch code.

10

THE PHILOSOPHY OF DOOM

PENCIL BETWEEN HIS TEETH, SCHATTEN was on the edge of his seat, scanning over the next segment as he had just left the portion of the script where the sub waited for the final order and the destruction of the world. He was poised looking for further details on the submarine, but the casual reference to the land-based missile launch was in the back of his mind since the previous text had only briefly alluded to it. But he didn't have to go far to find it, for now the other menacing head of von Weir's dragon made its appearance. Schatten would have to counter both contingencies. Von Weir's philosophy was simple: he reasoned that both China and Russia had always targeted the US with their respective arsenals. Each anticipated the day when the US would launch a preemptive strike, justifying a full response.

It would take little in the way of provocation to light the fuse. Once nuclear warheads impacted either nation and the monitoring devices of both counties confirmed that the aggressor was the United States, total nuclear war would be inevitable. Once the first shots were fired, no one would spend any time questioning the merits of retaliation; it would purely be a matter of survival. None would look around the world stage to see who was responding; everyone would be fighting for their very existence using whatever means necessary.

Once the bar was raised and the nuclear gloves were off, no one could stop it. Von Weir alone would have the clear vantage point, knowing what had really transpired, as chaos reigned. Once attacked, he envisioned the US response to be swift and devastating. They would launch all of their land-based arsenal and bombers and then command the submarine force to take care of the rest. The trick would be for the US and Soviet navies to annihilate one another.

To assure mutual destruction, Setski would sink at least one submarine from each fleet and use the chameleon device to provide the signature of an American vessel to the Russians and that of a Russian to the Americans. But he had to ensure that the Chinese were destroyed, for they alone had the ground forces to block his takeover. Once the nuclear arsenals of both the US and Russia were exhausted, it would get down to conventional warfare, and only China possessed the unlimited resources in terms of manpower. He had to make certain that they were in the middle of the fray to such a degree that all their land forces would be eliminated by both the Soviets and the West.

His worst fear would be for these Communist superpowers to unite against the West. So, to leave nothing to chance, he would have to ensure that missiles were launched from a Russian land-based site upon China. This would foster the illusion that Russia had aligned itself with the West and revive the simmering hatred that had always been there between their Chinese archrivals.

So, to preclude any possibility of an alliance, von Weir would not rely on one commandeered submarine to instigate hostilities. Instead, he would unleash his special force contingent to capture a Russian ICBM complex on the fringes of what was once the Soviet Union. He would target a facility in a remote sector of the continent where security was the weakest. But fully understanding the enormity of capturing such a facility, von Weir had placed a mole inside the complex like a Trojan horse; someone who would open the gates to his invaders when required. Thus, the second phase of the execution for world domination began to unfold.

Schatten, pencil in hand, furiously made notes on every sheet that described the complex.

He circled every page that discussed the facility and referenced other pages.

It was obvious that Karamov was privy to the intricacies of the Soviet military installations presented in this segment. Extreme detail highlighting even the ducting used in the environmental control system was evident.

Schatten made notes on these details for further reference as possible areas to exploit. The code name for the targeted facility was Akaba, an isolated missile complex on the boarder of Uzbekistan near the town of Tashkent. It was a best-kept Russian secret. It presented an innocuous appearance and was so secluded that no one would guess its true function. It operated under the guise of a weather research center, and the local populous were paid to keep up the deception.

It housed twenty-five long-range nuclear missiles capable of reaching anywhere on the globe and was designed to sustain a direct nuclear strike and survive. It was envisioned that the elaborate subterfuge would label it a non-target by US strategists.

Schatten continued to read the details, and it made his skin crawl. The attack force was composed of a core of twenty highly trained and highly paid ex-Soviet Special Forces. They were supplemented by twenty additional troops comprised of Arab fanatics who served as cannon fodder to allow the elite force to conduct the business of capturing, holding, and operating the complex until the entire arsenal had been launched. Their infiltrator provided a detailed layout of the facility and played a key role. He would smuggle in an oxygen bottle containing a highly lethal nerve gas. It was so potent that unless special gear was worn, anyone exposed to it in any fashion would succumb to its devastating effects in mere minutes.

The operation was scheduled to start at 2100 hours and well ahead of the positioning of the submarine. It was the first time that Karamov had mentioned a timeline, and Schatten thought that disrupting the schedule might create a weakness that would render the plot harmless. Von Weir hoped that the assault on the complex would eventually bring the Russians to full alert status. This would serve to mask the taking of the submarine, for their focus would be elsewhere.

A secret tunnel used for emergency evacuation served as the entrance to the bunker. The assault would begin when the infiltrator commanding one of the launch stations left his post. This coincided with a regular scheduled break to reduce the effects of fatigue and allow the men to relieve themselves. The lethal container was housed with other oxygen bottles, which were used for emergency contingencies and frequently replaced to ensure their proper operation. The entire complex had back-up air filtration and water purification in the event of nuclear, chemical, or biological attack. To breach this system was a daunting task without the infiltrator.

The traitor's first assignment was to navigate down several tunnels that snaked through the underground fortress until he arrived at the station that controlled the power to the outer escape tunnel door. Opening the massive outer hatch, which was designed to repel even a direct nuclear hit, the attack force would enter the tunnel. Now, they faced a second door that could not be opened without triggering an alarm at every level. This smaller inner hatch was the only thing separating the intruders from the inhabitants within the complex. The attackers would place shaped charges atop the hatch and destroy the locking mechanism. The charges provided minimal noise due to the massive insulation surrounding the door and they would destroy the electrical circuitry, meaning that no detection was possible. This was the assault for which the Russians and Arabs had trained previously.

Once his first task was complete, the conspirator would rush back to the area where the spare oxygen was stored. Retrieving his contaminated container, he donned a bio-chemical mask, which was standard issue to this unit. Taking the container to the latrine, he would open an air duct and place the bottle inside. Next, he would open the valve, releasing the volatile agent.

Unbeknownst to the man, his accomplices failed to notify him that a special suit was required to protect him. The deadly c1234 agent, as coded by the Russian Army Biological Warfare Institute, was at the top of the lethality chart. It could be transmitted by air or contact and only required an exposure time of ten seconds to kill anything within twenty-five meters. It would have been painfully obvious that his men had planned to betray him all along. He had been sacrificed to prevent any trail if the operation was unsuccessful.

Schatten thought that this could be a beautiful flaw if the mole was alerted to his suicide mission. He quickly jotted down the name of the bioweapon and the individual who was to release it.

Percussion grenades would rip through the silence as the invaders, clothed in the proper biogear, would enter with a vengeance. They would systematically sweep through the entire complex, pausing to ensure that every compartment was saturated with the toxin and every man was dead. Meters strapped to their wrists would indicate the level of toxicity. Soon, they would be in command of the entire operation . . . and, only moments after, would find the safe containing the launch codes and activation keys.

After the messy work of piling up the bodies and removing them from their respective stations, the attackers would assume their launch positions. Once the base was secured, the outer hatch was to be closed, and the code word "Everest" transmitted to von Weir.

"What if the outer hatch becomes disabled?" thought Schatten out loud as he scribbled more notes on disrupting Karamov.

Von Weir would now send back his confirmation along with the code to standby. A specialist would reprogram each missile to strike China with a full salvo. Using the multiple warhead configurations atop each missile, he could attack all the major troop staging areas and their weaponry. The monitoring board inside the complex also tracked the limited array of Chinese ballistic missile submarines. This was a much easier task for the Russians than trailing US underwater vessels with their sophisticated stealth technology. Von Weir was much more concerned with the Chinese than he was the US or Russia. He reasoned that the Russians and Americans would destroy one another once war was declared. But he feared that the Chinese navy would go unscathed and serve as his only threat. Therefore, he would target these limited assets to assure their destruction. When the board indicated their demise and he was convinced that he, the US, and Russia had obliterated the Chinese military in general, he would launch the rest of the arsenal against the US.

With his land-based weaponry secured and his ocean-going arsenal in place, Von Weir needed only to dispatch the launch code to begin Armageddon, chaos, and the end of all sanity.

Schatten read on as all aspects of the operation were meticulously outlined in vivid detail down to the role of each participant. The intricate workings of his security system were revealed along with the economic resources involved. The terrorist alliance between his East and West extremists was shaky at best, but the commonality for each faction was power and wealth. The fact that the organized world was reduced to an unimaginable state where chaos reigned played into the hands of von Weir's rabble. For the religious zealots, it was a jihad—a holy war that cleansed the Eastern culture of Western domination.

To the Russian political extremists, it was a revamping of all that had gone wrong after wasted years, trying to emulate the western capitalists. To the criminal element, anarchy meant authority and their chance to remake their respective societies in their own twisted image and spread their tentacles into every sector. They could offer any diversion imagined to the suffering and downtrodden for a hefty profit.

Everyone involved in this sordid enterprise had no doubts that their efforts would be recouped. The Arab terrorists hoped to corner the Mideast oil market, using their newfound muscle.

Most of the Earth would be devastated, but countries and continents like Africa, the

Philippines, Australia, and South America could remain habitable, although gripped by the effects of nuclear winter and radiation. But no matter the outcome, the promise of power transcended religious and political affiliations.

As von Weir so adeptly pointed out to his confidant, Ian Androkov, "Mask it in whatever guises you like; power and its associated evils are the milk to nurturing megalomaniacs, and it will continue as long as there are those who will allow themselves to be subjugated."

With his submarine poised to devastate the United States and Britain and his massive ICBM complex in tow, von Weir knew that he had already done the impossible.

Disgusted, Schatten had been scribbling notes continuously during his reading of Karamov's story, noting possible weaknesses. Flaws with the Chameleon device, inherent weaknesses in various systems, and betrayal of the mole and others seemed like a good start.

Schatten lamented that he had not entered the classified database until now. But he had put it off long enough. He stepped out onto the small deck of the beach house to clear his head. After taking a few long, slow breaths in the ocean air, he came to his senses and was up to the task. He now knew the full extent of the plan.

11
UNDOING ARMAGEDDON

SCHATTEN GRABBED ALL HIS NOTES AND marked-up copy regarding the submarine and the missile complex. It was time for Schatten to find a way to unravel this morbid plot now indelibly etched in his mind. He learned to avoid getting bogged down in the massive details and concentrate on exploiting the plot's weaknesses. It was his job to derail the plan. The time had come to enter the classified system. He could not avoid the prospect any longer.

With great trepidation, he sat down at the keyboard and looked at the codebook for the website that the good professor had presented him. Schatten organized his notes to follow to ensure that his limited time within the database was as productive as possible. He connected the internet line and then thought about the consequences of being discovered and the time limitations imposed. Schatten had initially considered traveling to a public place such as a library in case something went wrong, and he had to escape. But he knew that he would constantly be looking over his shoulder to see if anyone was watching. Since he was paranoid enough about this situation, he opted to enter the portal from the privacy of his beach house.

He set the timer on his radio clock for one hour and then entered the first of the series of passwords that Chelston had given him. Each contained thirty-two digits with small and capital letters and characters interspersed between numbers in random order. The computer was set up to recognize the codes and automatically connect to a classified website after the entire password was typed in, followed by the *Enter* button.

No sooner had his finger hit *Enter* than the screen featured an intimidating message in bold crimson letters warning of fine and imprisonment, signifying that this was a highly restricted site for official government use only. This struck fear into Schatten, but he persevered. He navigated through four separate firewalls, each utilizing different passwords, before he entered the "vault," as the professor had called it. Now he was faced with a screen so cluttered that he had a hard time concentrating on a particular topic. But he had to steer his way through in order to locate some type of index or search button. When he found the term *Find* stuffed into the upper right-hand corner of the screen, he typed in the words "Soviet submarines" and waited for the response.

In a fraction of a second, a screen appeared, alive with data categories, featuring a cornucopia of topics. There were categories for all classes of ships, but the word submarine was highlighted. He clicked on this offering, which led to another screen with every country represented that possessed such a vessel. When he spotted the words Russia/Soviet Union in highlights, he immediately activated that selection. Every conceivable type of submersible was covered. He paged down the list until the class of ship described in the Karamov's text emerged. A three-dimensional picture of the craft appeared that he could view from any angle. Every conceivable system of the ship was shown and color-coded.

By placing his cursor on a category such as electrical, the entire wiring schematic of the vessel could be seen, along with every component that comprised the system. Thinking quickly, he looked for anything on the system's vulnerabilities. There was another search feature that he utilized; he typed in *failure modes*, but nothing happened. Then he typed in *vulnerabilities*. The words *Retrieving Data* flashed on the screen. He waited impatiently until a list of items appeared.

Two of the items had the abbreviation *SPF* attached in parentheses. *What is that?* he thought. He placed the cursor on the abbreviation and pressed the mouse button. Suddenly, the phrase *Single Point Failure* appeared. Although not skilled in the design of complex military systems, he had an engineering degree and understood that the term "single point failure" meant the Achilles' heel of the system. Simply put, it was a single weakness, whereby the malfunction of a lone component could bring down an entire system. This was a feature that all good engineers strove to avoid at all costs during the design phase and something he was hoping to exploit now.

Schatten highlighted both items and clicked the mouse. The screen scrolled down immediately and the word *Working* flashed in the upper left-hand corner. Then a cross section of the vessel was shown with points highlighted with green circles. He put his curser on one of the circles in the bow of the ship and pressed the mouse. A piping schematic was shown with two valves highlighted. He hit the word

Description listing the flaws in one particular valve. It showed its function, failure mode, reliability, and the effect of its malfunction on the operation of the entire ship. The body of the valve was changed from aluminum to titanium when it was discovered that the valve would melt when exposed to elevated temperatures.

Another of the flawed components located at the center of the vessel was a pump used to dispense fire retardant to an area housing numerous wire bundles.

Suddenly, the alarm clock sounded, signifying that he had to get out now. Furiously trying to locate the *Exit* button, Schatten panicked. In desperation, he grabbed the power cord and ripped it from the wall.

Breathing heavily, he sat staring at the dark screen for several minutes. Berating himself for his childish response, he would give himself ample time to leave the classified system properly. Regaining his composure, he began to look at his notes, scribbled in desperation. His inability to use the printer while inside the classified database challenged his memory, as his powers of recollection were sorely lacking. But there was nothing he could do, he had to play by Chelston's rules. He had to rely on his notes and sketches and reenter the system only if it was necessary. He plugged the computer back in and sat down in front of the screen.

Soon, he began to compose the storyline to defeat Karamov's submission. He began pounding away at the keyboard until he had the outline of his story and all the most important data fused into the counterplot. Then he reviewed what he had in his possession from the Russian author to see where he would inject his additions.

Armed with the failure scenarios, Schatten could totally disable the vessel. As he wrote, fleshing in the details and making corrections, he scribbled notes on the Russian's pages where his changes would be inserted, while jotting down which pages required removal. Chelston had told him that he could not reenter the database until a minimum of one hour had passed. So, he concentrated on what he had already learned.

He continued to write for several hours before looking at the clock. Four more hours had passed, his eyes were heavy, and his stomach needed food. Schatten put a TV dinner into the microwave and went for a walk on the beach. After skipping a few rocks and feeling the warm ocean surf on his feet, he went back into the beach house and consumed his meal.

He looked at the clock once more—5:26 p.m.—the hours seemed to vanish in a flash. Schatten had already written what he perceived as a sure-fire script to cause the sub to become inoperable by using the failed valve and pump scenarios. But Schatten had a nagging fear in the back of his mind that his changes to Karamov's storyline might be rejected for any number of nebulous reasons.

This lack of confidence had been Schatten's constant companion and one need only look at his father as the cause. He was always critical of everything his son did and the mental scars were still there. They would manifest themselves in high-pressure situations where he was suddenly overcome by that "you're not good enough" feeling. So, to put his mind at ease, he needed a backup plan—an alternate storyline just in case.

In this scenario, he would target von Weir's mysterious device, the Chameleon. He reentered the database to search for the vulnerability of the cloaking device, the key element in Karamov's story. He remembered that Chelston had told him that one of the rules was that one could not refer to a piece of technology that did not already exist. Therefore, if the all-encompassing database did not show its existence, he must assume that it was only a product of the Russian's imagination. It could not become reality, anyway, thus insuring that Karamov's plot was doomed from this fact alone. But if Schatten discovered that the Chameleon was viable, he had to find its flaws and exploit them as his fallback position. He searched at breakneck speed for the device and found a folder interesting enough labeled Chameleon. It was a small file and gave a short biography on the inventor and the hardware's capabilities. The intelligence told that the system did not demonstrate its proposed abilities and was cumbersome. It had to be installed into the ship's electrical system and caused major issues resulting in overloads and fires. It was rejected with scathing reviews by government and industry. It was labeled as dangerous and unstable. Schatten wrote at breakneck speed, capturing as much data as he could before the time expired.

He developed three storylines while they were fresh in his mind but settled on one for submission. It included the Chameleon, the pumps and valves as overkill.

Schatten wrote feverishly, trying to get all his thoughts down as quickly as possible. But there were scores of notes, so he created a brief outline to recall everything. He initially conceived of disabling the craft once it reached the depths of the North Atlantic. But then he thought that it might be better to have the failure occur in the harbor at Sevastopol. There, the disabled boat could be easily captured, along with her crew. This would insure minimum loss of life and no possibility of a missile being fired, stolen, or lost.

He wrote that as the captain took his position on the bridge, he addressed the entire crew and ordered the activation of the Chameleon. This caused an immediate surge in the electrical system, disabling half the bridge's consoles that monitored the various systems of the immense craft. As they searched the ship for the cause, smoke filled several of the passageways, as fires began to spread. It was the first real test of the redesigned cloaking system on a real ship and no accounting was made to upgrade any of the wiring. Setski had never been informed of this requirement, and it did not appear in the overhaul specifications. He ordered that respirators be distributed. The flames burned through the fire suppression pump's aluminum housing, not upgraded to titanium, due to funding shortages. Without the fire extinguishers, the flames spread unchecked. Pumps and valves providing coolant to the reactors now were becoming affected, and the core temperature approached the critical threshold. They were forced to shut down the entire power grid to repair and isolate the damage. After several minutes, it was clear that the ship attracted attention from those monitoring the harbor. A destroyer was dispatched to provide assistance. The crew had no choice now but to attempt an underwater escape. They assembled in the forward section of the ship and exited through the emergency hatches. They swam submerged long enough to be out of sight before the rescue crew could assess what had transpired. The rescue vessel soon called for emergency personnel and within a couple of minutes, the channel was crawling with men and ships. A rescue crew entered the ship but found no one aboard. This immediately sparked a manhunt for the crew and several members were caught and interrogated. The investigation grew, and everyone at the facility was questioned. All feigned innocence and told everything they knew, leading to a wave of finger pointing and betrayal. Executions and torture provided the inquisitors with all the missing pieces of the puzzle. After several days, all were captured or shot, and the plot began to unravel. The entire affair was totally suppressed by the FSB and seen as a source of embarrassment that would not be repeated. The only positive remnant of the whole affair was a massive effort by the Russians to properly secure all nuclear arms.

Pleased with his effort, Schatten now was ready to address the land-based operation. He entered the top-secret realm once more. He rummaged through the various offerings to find the search feature. Schatten soon found the listing of all the active Russian ICBM complexes. He had the name of the facility highlighted on a sheet from Karamov's text in front of him and paged down the list until he found it. Placing the cursor on the highlighted location, the system responded immediately with extensive information on the facility. It showed its exact geographic location and a three-dimensional lay of the land surrounding it. He noted that it was in a valley, making the base only accessible in one direction. Schatten summoned a three-dimensional internal map of the complex that could be rotated and viewed from multiple angles. He zoomed in to various sectors and saw graphic details of launch stations, storage areas, and other principle locations within the vast maze of bunkers described in the Russian's script. He traced the route that the traitor would take to accomplish his sabotage. Schatten made sketches of the sections of the facility that would provide him the means to counter Karamov's strategies.

Schatten's counterplot to foil the capture of the missile complex began by adding that unbeknownst to the men assaulting the facility, an informer leaked the plot some weeks before. Disgruntled by the lack of authority he was given in the new world order; this man would come forward after negotiating his immunity with the United States government and receiving payment for his testimony. The informer would outline the basics of the plan in enough detail to give the Russian government reason to scrutinize the plot. Although unclear as to the exact location of the attacks, the authorities nonetheless were alerted that such events would transpire.

Special Forces personnel were dispatched to several complexes to infiltrate the personnel. They posed as additional crew members and helped to install scores of sensing devices to detect any biological/chemical toxins. The latest in biochemical protection gear was dispatched to every ICBM complex. In addition, the latest in body armor was issued so that the entire suit would be covered to ensure that the ensemble could not be breached by automatic weapons fire. This provided the assurance that any attack would be stalled until additional forces were employed to annihilate the invaders. Highly mobile elite counter terrorist teams, specially trained to neutralize such threats, were on constant alert. Stationed at strategic locations, they would be deployed by helicopter at a moment's notice. An alarm system, installed as part of the new biochemical sensors, would immediately signal these forces when any biochemical agent was detected inside the complex. The system could also be activated manually if an attack occurred by pushing any one of several emergency buttons installed at key locations.

When members of the submarine's crew were captured, the pieces fell into place and the target's location pinpointed. Once this was done, the plan was for the special troops to mobilize immediately to foil the attack, hoping to kill or capture the entire force and leave no escape route.

Special measures were taken to ensure that the mole inside the complex was unaware of what was transpiring. Thus, the traitor was never alerted of any change in the number of personnel and viewed the replacements as a part of the standard rotation process in the high-pressure atmosphere. When the mole, Ivan Moldorkof, left to activate the outer hatch, hidden surveillance cameras were ready to pick up his every move. Before he could unleash the powerful toxin, he was captured and interrogated.

Subsequently, the terrorist troops amassed outside the complex were soon surrounded as they tried to set their explosives. Those that would not surrender were immediately gunned down, and those that ran were easy prey for tanks and circling attack helicopters. After the capture or death of all the conspirators, the

Russians secretly contacted members of the international community to aid in the capture of von Weir and his remaining henchmen. A combined antiterrorist unit from Russia, the United States, and the United Kingdom traced and captured them. Although squabbling took place over where they were to be tried, the Russians would win out, and the other nations conceded. Justice was quick, and the outcome, a forgone conclusion.

Now with the scenario complete, Schatten checked the rules of submission. It was explained that the exact location of each page's insertion must be provided along with the page numbers of the previous submittal, which required removal. Thus, Schatten was extremely careful to be precise as to how and where he would splice his text into the original story.

After the last page, Schatten placed "The End" at the bottom per the prescribed rules. This would now serve as the new final page of the story and terminate anything that Karamov had submitted. The only thing left was to perform the actual submission.

He had done it all and still had six days to spare. Schatten glowed with confidence and knew that if he did not commit any errors in typing during the submission that he would win out. He had turned man's last days into a new Genesis. Pleased with his accomplishments, he fell asleep at 11:51 p.m. as the first day concluded.

12
THE RULES HAVE CHANGED

SCHATTEN SLEPT WELL AND LAY ON THE couch for several minutes after awakening as the cobwebs left his head. He walked over to the window and looked out at the clear morning, listening to the waves roll up on the shore. He ventured outside to breath in the salt air and felt the warmth of the summer sun on his face.

"Hello, my friend. Beautiful morning, isn't it?" he said to a hermit crab scurrying to conceal itself in the sand. Several seagulls were screeching overhead, slowly circling, looking for a meal. He walked back inside to the refrigerator and removed a gallon container of orange juice and poured a glass.

After consuming a bowl of cereal, he went back to the business of researching Karamov's work.

He had to ensure that he had wreaked havoc with the Chameleon, the system to mask the identity of Setski's submarine. Now, all that remained was troubleshooting his laptop for any mistakes and transferring his writings to the typewriter. He'd thought he was finished when he went to bed, but now he realized that the process of transferring everything to the typewriter was not so simple. He read through what he had composed and searched for any anomalies.

Hours went by before he, again, looked at the clock and saw that it was 11:06 a.m. But he was obsessed with finishing his story, and so worked through lunch. Once he had it down, he stopped briefly to go to the bathroom and get himself a drink. Then, he went about the business of additional polishing of the text and weeding out all the spelling and grammatical errors.

By the time he stopped, it was 5:37 p.m. He knew he had to rest for a moment and get something to eat but wanted to complete the proofed version of the story. When the writer was confident that he had it all in its final form, he decided to go over it one more time, leaving nothing to chance. Using the spell check application inside the word processor program, he searched for any irregularities denoted by red underlining and reread all forty-one pages. Schatten hadn't intended to write that much but felt compelled to be as meticulous as possible, mimicking the style of the Russian, as Chelston had suggested. Then, he went over the pages that he had marked in Karamov's text where he would inject his text and the sections that would be eliminated. He then reviewed his spreadsheet that showed exactly where each page of his text would mesh into Karamov's storyline. This served as his outline when typing his changes into the typewriter. It would help him keep track and assure that he missed nothing. Lastly, he decided to make a hardcopy of his composition and mark each line after he had typed it.

Looking at the clock once more, he saw that it was now 8:55 p.m. and that the sun was beginning to set. He rubbed his neck, stood up, and stretched. He still hadn't eaten anything and could scarcely believe that he had wasted an entire day merely rewriting his text. Schatten shoved a TV dinner into the microwave once more and set the timer. He ventured outside to see the majestic sunset illuminate the sky like a giant prism.

"It'll all be over in a couple more hours," he said out load, as if to reassure himself. But he had thought the same thing yesterday and twenty-four hours had elapsed.

He was beginning to feel the stress of the many hours that he had poured into the work with only one break. It was now an obsession to finish off the story by entering it into the mysterious device that portrayed itself as a normal typewriter. He filled his lungs with the salt air once more and watched the sun descend behind the horizon. Schatten returned to the house, turning on the lights and TV while he ate his meal. Then he switched the TV off and went into the bathroom and looked at his face in the mirror. Schatten turned on the cold tap and doused his face with a handful of water and then proceeded to walk over to the typewriter. He switched on the table lamp and placed his text beside the unit. Schatten had marked each page of his text with the exact page number and line from the Russian's novel into which his offering would be placed. The monitor displayed the spreadsheet that he would mark by typing an X into the column with the header "Complete" as each page was painstakingly typed on the keyboard. Schatten was starting to become fatigued now but endured as his adrenaline pumped furiously. He was extremely nervous as his fingers pressed the first few keys of the old machine. It was a strange sensation, using this ancient unit to copy a text that he had composed on its contemporary counterpart. It was like playing without a safety net, for he would not know if he had made an error until the SAM computer informed him of such. If this occurred, according to Chelston, he would be required to retype it all once more, only knowing what the error was from the rejection code, but only in general terms. One missed keystroke could make all the difference. He pecked away on the keyboard slowly, painstakingly, and methodically, looking at every stroke he entered to ensure that he had not made an error. As he got further into the submittal, the tension amplified. As the typed pages stacked up, he read each one as he slipped in a new sheet. It was as though he were blindfolded walking a tightrope. One missed step and it was all over. The further he proceeded, the more the opportunity for error intensified. Looking at the outline and the printout, he went about the excruciating process of telling the SAM computer which lines to eliminate and which to add. His hands now began to shake as he entered the final lap of the marathon. He intertwined his fingers and stretched out his arms as far as he could to alleviate the tension. Schatten kept driving and pressuring himself until finally, he had come to the end of the ordeal.

He quickly scanned every sheet of paper that he had inserted into the typewriter as a record of every keystroke and to look for any obvious mistakes. Seeing none, Schatten held his breath as he hit the send button. It was anticlimactic in a way, but it was finished. Now he could only sit and wait to see if his offering had been accepted or unceremoniously rejected.

Schatten looked up at the clock once more and noted that it was 11:01 p.m. He was totally drained after the experience but found solace that it all might be over before this day would end. Then he could bank his money from Chelston and finish his novel. It could be as simple as that. He'd get rid of the typewriter and go back to the gloriously mundane.

Switching on the television once more, he lay on the couch and used the remote control to search for a movie. One station was carrying a John Wayne marathon, and he gladly reclined and relaxed. Soon the pressure of the day began to abate, and his eyes began to close as exhaustion overtook him. He slept for just over four hours when he awoke to the sound of the printer, which suddenly became alive with text. Startled by the sound, he rose to his feet and fumbled in the darkened room, illuminated only by the light from the television, and walked to the machine.

"What is this?" he said out loud, totally confused.

Then he looked at the typewriter that now featured a glowing green light that permeated the darkness on the side of the machine.

"It's been accepted!" he shouted in exuberance. "My story's been accepted. I won, it's over!"

But his celebration was cut short as he switched on the light and began to read through the confusing text now coming in waves off the printer. As he read on, it was obvious that it was from Karamov.

"Is this new stuff?" he muttered. "It can't be . . . How?"

He grabbed page after page and scanned each one before picking up the first page of his own work. Schatten had to know if his own insertions were part of what he was reading. The writer looked at the pages being received by the computer. To his horror, Schatten saw that they mirrored his additions with subtle changes. It was as though the Russian had been in the room with him, looking over his shoulder. Scrutinizing each page as it came off the printer, it was obvious that Karamov was attempting to undo everything that Schatten had done. He was rewriting his own book and circumventing every obstacle that Schatten had thrown in his path.

"He knows what I'm doing!" Schatten shouted. "He can see what I'm writing!"

But how could this be? He had to call Chelston now, no matter what the hour. He looked for Chelston's number, picked up the phone, and quickly dialed the number. He waited as ten rings ensued before someone finally picked up the phone.

"Hello," said a voice in slurred speech, obviously drowsy.

"Hello, Dr. Chelston, is that you?"

"Yes, this is Chelston. Who's calling please?"

"Professor, it's me, Mike Schatten. I have to speak to you."

"What is this about, young man? Do you know what time it is?" he replied, yawning.

"Yes, I'm sorry to disturb you, but things are happening that you told me couldn't!" shouted Schatten.

"Calm down, dear boy, just tell me what happened," said Chelston calmly.

"Well, I submitted my storyline, and the computer accepted it. At least I think it did," said Schatten.

"Is there a green light illuminating on the left front of the unit?" asked Chelston.

"Yes."

"Good work, my boy, you've done it. So what's the problem?" replied the professor.

"But after it was approved, I began receiving more text . . . from Karamov," said Schatten.

"Are you certain? Are you sure that you weren't printing some of the old text instead?"

"No, it's not my work. The style is definitely his. But it's as though he read everything that I submitted. Professor, he knows what I'm doing.

You told me that was impossible since my typewriter is the only one capable of receiving."

"How long ago did you submit your work?" asked Chelston.

"Ah, I don't know. What time is it?" he said glancing at the clock. "Three, maybe four hours ago," replied Schatten.

"Okay, how long after the green light appeared did you start receiving this new script?" asked Chelston.

"I can't say exactly, I fell asleep shortly after I sent it, around 11 p.m.," replied Schatten. "It's like he responded immediately, as though he was receiving everything I submitted. Otherwise, how could he respond that fast? Karamov altered the pages I submitted. He undid everything I wrote."

"Let's assume that it was approved within an hour of your submittal," said Chelston. "That would have given him roughly three hours to write the material and respond. How many pages has he submitted?"

"So far, there are, I don't know, fifty sheets?" Schatten responded.

"Well this is curious. He shouldn't possess that capability. I don't understand this at all," said the professor. "But in any event, stay calm, my boy."

"So, what do we do now?" asked Schatten.

"It appears the rules have changed. Looks like your joust with the master is not just a single event, so to speak. It appears now that this might be a series of matches. Apparently, his unit was upgraded before it left for England. We must assume that he has your capabilities now. Yes, the rules have changed, my boy. Tell me, what is the new text like?" said the professor.

"It appears to be the same plot, only modified to undo what I submitted. What do I do now?" asked Schatten.

"Submit another change to his story and see how quickly he responds. But he can't submit the same exact story twice; that would violate the rules, you see," said Chelston.

"But he could alter it, right?" asked the writer.

"That seems to be the case. We're sailing through unchartered waters, I'm afraid," responded the professor. "We must see what he's capable of before we can undermine his plot. The good news is that you have one major advantage over our friend."

"What's that?" asked Schatten.

"He must respond to *you*. Let's see how fast he reacts," said Chelston. "Michael you must submit several scenarios and see how quickly he adjusts. If it took three hours last time we must discern how quickly he is receiving your text. In any event, compose more stories based upon his counter plots and submit them as quickly as you can, but toss in something new to throw him off."

"I already had a backup story in case my first was rejected," said Schatten.

"Good, submit that as quickly as you can and keep tabs on how fast he counters. Think of it this way, you are in command now, and it's he who is countering your moves on the chessboard. Keep me appraised, Michael," said Chelston and hung up the phone.

Schatten looked at the clock and noted that it was 4:54 a.m. Two days had passed, and he was back to square one. He began to read through everything that had come off the printer and compared each page of the Russian's new text with his. As he went over each change, he noted that his adversary hadn't done anything dramatically new, other than offer minute variations. It was suddenly apparent that he had hardly altered what Schatten had written other than to simply undo the changes. When Schatten wrote that inferior wiring was used, the Russian countered that all the wiring had been upgraded, specifically to allow for the application of the Chameleon. Karamov then added details of the ship's overhaul, stipulating that everything was tested before the ship embarked so that nothing was left to chance. He then added back all the sections that Schatten had removed regarding the nuclear conflict and von Weir's ascension to power. This confused Schatten at first for Chelston had assured him that nothing previously submitted could be done so again. So Schatten began intently analyzing Karamov's latest work and noted the subtle differences from the previous. The

Russian was still presenting the same plot only with minute variations, just enough to thwart Schatten's intervention. In any event, he was ready to submit his alternate plan to defeat the aggressors from taking over the ICBM complex and then seal the fate of the submarine. He was reeling from lack of sleep and went into the bathroom and splashed cold water on his face. Looking in the mirror, he uttered, "Here we go again," and shook his head. Now he retrieved his backup storyline that he withheld in case the SAM had rejected his previous offering.

Schatten wrote that the assault on the complex started as planned by the terrorists. Entering the fortress through the outer hatch and scaling down the steep steps leading to the first escape tunnel, they quickly stormed through the underground facility. They searched for survivors and checked their monitoring devices to ensure that the atmosphere had been completely saturated with the toxin. But the devices failed to register anything. Undaunted, they charged into the bunker complex. They would see no bodies, for the mole had betrayed them. The double agent would now close the outer hatch trapping the attackers inside. He had also flooded the passageways with teargas, simulating the real toxin and severely impairing their vision. As the attacking force continued through the darkened inner passages, they grew ever closer to the main control station at the center of the complex. They ran in waves, each intruder serving to back up the other. Their dark green camouflage was almost unrecognizable in the dim atmosphere in the bowels of the structure, permeated by the nonlethal mist. Using hand signals to overcome the poor reception of their communication systems, each room was assaulted. Relentlessly, they pursued the command station and its bounty of lethal missiles, totally unaware of the trap awaiting them. They were now in the control room and about to override the system when they were met by sudden flashes of light, signifying a volley of heavy gunfire. Three of the assailants went down instantaneously as the bullets from the automatic weapons penetrated their suits, skillfully wheeled by the Russian special forces.

The attackers were totally unaware that a contingent of elite fighters had infiltrated the compound during a period of several months. The smoke-filled atmosphere was compounded from the discharges of the terrorists' gunfire as the ear-piercing sounds from their weapons echoed off the concrete walls. The defenders soon deployed smoke canisters as further additions to the untenable atmosphere. Even though the invaders wore night vision goggles, the heavy atmosphere disrupted their ability to navigate, and they were unaware that they were being caught in a crossfire. The Russians had maneuvered through secret passages inside the walls of the tunnels to encircle them. The initiative was now with the defenders, and the invaders could only drop to the floor and try to regroup. Every second was paramount now as it was clear that the plan had been seriously compromised. The silent alarm system had automatically activated immediately after the teargas was vented into the environment. It soon brought the introduction of hordes of elite Soviet anti-terrorist troops stationed nearby, who were more than a match for the small group of mercenaries. Overwhelmed by sheer numbers, as well as the quality of the forces amassed against them, they had no choice but to surrender or die. Totally unable to regain their bearings and under the delusion that any wound meant an imminent and horrible death, the ranks began to collapse as several of the terrorists were taken hostage. Between the efficient utilization of mind-altering drugs, sleep deprivation, and torture, the Russians soon learned the major details behind the plot, especially the hijacking of the missile submarine.

An immediate emergency call was put out to the entire fleet to respond and to conduct an inventory. A count was made of every vessel in the fleet and its location immediately transmitted to a central command center. An electronic spreadsheet was quickly created to give an accounting of each vessel and its whereabouts. The only ship that was missing was that commandeered by the revolutionaries. The guards at the naval facility were hunted down as a relentless search was conducted for each. An incredible manhunt ensued for everyone even remotely related to the vessel. Every worker, technician and individual having the slightest knowledge of the craft was detained and questioned by whatever means necessary. Families were threatened and executions were promised to anyone who would not cooperate. As the various participants were rounded up, new pieces of the puzzle were uncovered, and a portrait of alarming scope began to emerge. As the technicians responsible for installing the secret stealth device were discovered, the intricate workings of the system came to light. The American Navy was solicited to avail itself in hunting down the renegade underwater vessel and the pirates who had stolen it. The Americans cooperated all too gladly when told of the extensiveness of the plot. It was their sophisticated listening arrays which provided the ability to screen the sounds emanating from the hunted ship and pinpoint its location. Although they would not be party to its sinking, they would help corner the ship and lead the hounds to it. They would then standoff while it was sunk or boarded. The men of the US attack submarines, and surface vessels understood the seriousness of the job at hand and wanted to ensure that not a single missile from the renegade left its tube. But, like treeing a wounded bear, they knew the dangers inherent in such operations. But they gladly risked their lives for the stability of the world and the chance to save humanity. Eventually, the rogue ship was driven to one of the deepest trenches in the Atlantic. There, the crew was given the ultimatum to surrender or die. The slightest provocative act by the prey, whether an outer torpedo door opening or a missile hatch's activation, would bring a hail of more concentrated underwater weaponry than any craft had ever faced. There would be no escape and no way out of their demise. The Russians would use any weapon necessary to neutralize the boat. Several discussions were conducted between high-ranking naval officers and political officials over the fate of the vessel. One faction wanted to make an example of the ship by its obliteration. Some wanted to save the craft and the millions of rubles that would be lost if it met its demise. Others wanted merely to meter out the maximum penalty to each member, but not before interrogating each to learn every sordid detail by the most diabolical methods possible. But such discussions would only serve to prolong the life of the boat's crew. The major issue was not to allow the launch of any of its arsenal. Although the Russians hadn't disclosed all the despicable events being played out in this macabre game of cat and mouse, the stakes were too high not to. If missiles were launched at China, no matter the alibi, there could be hell to pay. By the same token the US would not be placated in the least if New York or Washington, D.C., was blown off the map.

The crew was given two minutes to make its decision. Each circling aircraft, attack sub, and surface vessel had crew members poised with fingers on the triggers of their respective weapons.

Below, Setski had ordered all aboard the fateful submarine to refrain from any activity and that all remain silent. He sat quietly, playing his mind games like a chess master surveying the board, constantly running scenarios through his brain, jotting down stroke and counter stroke. He took inventory of his torpedoes and theorized that if he detonated his nuclear warheads judiciously, he may be able to cause enough chaos to make his escape. If he took out the Americans, he might stand a better chance of eluding the less sophisticated listening arrays of the Russian fleet. Minutes seemed like hours as he stroked his chin, trying to decide. The faces of his men told of their apprehension and fear.

    Setski knew his next course of action. He ordered the boat to travel at maximum speed in a straight bow down maneuver. Throwing caution to the wind, he would take his craft to a depth that would make him impervious to their assault. The risk of crushing the hull would be weighed against the sheer destructive power amassed against him and the spirits of the men whose fate he held. For even if this outlandish mission failed, he could still know in his heart that he did his utmost to save the lives of his men. Now he must foster their trust that he would lead them out of the shadow of death.

The ship turned abruptly, and its diving planes gripped the icy water, thrusting it steadily to unimagined depths. The crews of the surface vessels and other underwater craft soon were alerted to the maneuver. Setski was banking on the fact that such a radical move would lead to moments of indecision, which could allow him to pull off his escape. He counted upon the faith of his men and the ability to arrogantly outthink his pursuers to pull him through. If he could make it to the bottomless trench below, he could use it as possible cover to mask his escape. He would discharge every counter measure he had available and detonate a nuclear torpedo if necessary.

Once his plan had manifested itself, the captains of each Russian vessel conferred immediately as to the next action. They had set up a conference capability for such a contingency tied in with the hierarchy in the Kremlin. Each second of indecision was one less opportunity to stop the aggressor. The total depth of the area was immediately discussed as well as the options and the ordinance of choice to terminate their rogue craft.

A furious discussion ensued regarding who should take the initiative and fire the first shot and how effective each weapon would be. Must they use a strictly conventional approach or should they play the nuclear option? Time was running out, and the Americans bristled at the indecision. They had already mapped their strategy and couldn't tolerate a single minute more of the perceived ineptness. But this was precisely what Setski had envisioned, and they were playing into his hands.

The captain of the attack submarine Dakota voiced the opinion that one of the attack subs should pursue Setski immediately. The depth readings were being relayed in ten-second intervals.

The decision was made to pursue to a prescribed depth and then fire fully armed nuclear torpedoes. Two Soviet subs, the Leningrad, and the Gorky, set out at flank speed to proceed to a sufficient depth to launch and detonate their weapons. The Dakota would follow to confirm the locations of both fox and hounds and map the undersea topography to ensure no collisions occurred. The superior speed of the attack subs allowed them to pull within range of the Typhoon. The Dakota kept transmitting a constant stream of data to both attacking ships to ensure they absolutely knew their position relative to the prey. In addition, each of the pursuing vessels was provided their distance from the canyon walls of the seemingly, bottomless trench. When they were in range, the order was given for both vessels to discharge their weapons. Four torpedoes were launched at specific intervals, each homing in on the sounds given off by the Typhoon's drive system. Setski discharged his array of counter measures hoping to deflect some of the weaponry hotly pursuing him. Then he fired two torpedoes from the stern tubes and set them to detonate as soon as the attacker's four weapons came in range. It would be a question whether or not his weapon deployment could defeat those crashing down on his craft. He was unaware that all four of the ordinances were nuclear, but he knew that his were. The attacking boats broke off the chase and headed toward the surface at full speed.

The other vessels cleared the blast zone as the weapons proceeded downward into what was hoped to be the tomb of the renegade launch platform.

The countdown began as the ships tried to remove themselves from harm's way. They had seen the weapons discharged by the enemy craft and all surmised that he, too, was playing for keeps and would play his nuclear trump card. As the clock ticked down and the attacking vessels ran for their lives, the Sonar arrays of all the vessels saw the detonations. The blast was tremendous, immediately sending shockwaves in all directions. The Typhoon could not outmaneuver the effects of the blast and crashed into the side of the trench as it continued steadily downward into the depths. The rudder caromed off a sharp ledge as the boat was rocked from stem to stern and the crew thrown against the walls of the ship. The massive electromagnetic energy bursting from the detonations destroyed many of the electronic circuits. The crew had totally lost the ability to steer due to the extensive damage incurred. Setski had no choice but to hold his position and listen to the sounds emanating from the surface. His only hope was to make them think that he was dead. But, for all intents and purposes, that was exactly what he was. Unable to reach the surface and unable to dive, he could only survive as long as his reactors would breathe life into the ship, but they couldn't manufacture food. He had stowed several months' supply of rations, but how long would it be before the pursuers would leave the area thinking that they had caused the craft's demise? The same question went through the minds of all that had taken part in the exercise on the surface.

The massive radiation levied on the surrounding seas would make any lengthy stay in the general vicinity impossible. They would leave buoys equipped with listening and video gear to record any sign of the vessel. Any trace would alert long range and carrier-based aircrafts that would be dispatched immediately to write the final chapter. For now, the entire fleet and all their crews would require massive decontamination. But such contingencies would not be necessary for Setski as the fate of the Typhoon was sealed. Unable to maneuver and having taken on a huge amount of contaminated seawater from breaches in the hull caused by the blasts, the boat began to sink. Pumps could not contain the damage, and ultimately, the vessel ventured into reaches beyond her designed limits. The listening devices would record her death knells some three days later. This sealed the book on the last of the terrorists and wrote the epitaph on the attempt to usurp the strength and prestige of the world's most powerful nations.

The plot began to unravel when a full investigation ensued at the facility where the boat had been overhauled and refitted. The extent of the corruption soon became apparent when almost every intelligence official, inspector, and worker seemed to be involved in some form or another. Banking records revealed large deposits in numerous individual accounts of those brazen enough not to care that the graft could be traced. Others, who hid the money, merely lied about their involvement but found that the circumstantial evidence was too compelling against them. They were all tried for treason and executed as examples to anyone in the future who would entertain any notion of repeating this sort of activity. Since terrorism was involved, no one in the world community would question the harshness of the punitive measures handed down. A cooperative effort between the US, Russia, China, and Europe was organized to track down all the conspirators.

13

THE NAME OF THE GAME

SCHATTEN WAS EXHAUSTED BY HIS LAST composition. He had to know what he was up against now. He'd been given the ground rules previously, but apparently, those boundaries didn't apply any more. But what was the name of the game now? What could his opponent's machine do, and was he privy to everything that Schatten composed? He needed to know if Karamov was indeed seeing

Revisionist Future

everything that he was submitting and in what timeline? Deep down, Schatten sensed that something was amiss but thought that the whole thing had been so absurd from the outset that this should have been expected.

He sensed that Karamov's machine could do more than his. But he would find out how fast the Russian was receiving his information, for Schatten was about to give Karamov another salvo.

Using the same method employed previously, Schatten typed and retyped his story on the word processor until it was polished to his satisfaction. He laboriously looked for every discrepancy and then printed out a hardcopy. Then he made another spreadsheet and marked where every insertion would take place and noted every page of the Russian's latest offering that would be deleted or replaced. Hours went by as he painstakingly amassed his work and placed it by the typewriter. He nervously looked at the clock and noted that it was 1:17 p.m. His stomach was growling, and his throat was dry, but he was obsessed with getting this second revision online and into the system via the magical keyboard. Proceeding as he had previously, looking at every keystroke and every page, Schatten was paranoid that he would make a mistake.

He pounded away at the keyboard for two more hours until he had finished the entire text and then hit the send button once more. Schatten was curious just how fast the SAM computer would deliver the decision whether his storyline met its approval. He had not been awake to see the previous green light's activation. Now, he stood up and stretched, then rubbed the back of his neck and arched his back. Schatten nervously began to pace the floor, waiting for the mysterious mega computer to render its decision. He decided to make a sandwich and opened a jar of peanut butter and retrieved the bread from the cupboard. Then he poured a glass of milk, sat down at the kitchen table, and stared at the typewriter.

It's like watching the proverbial boiling pot, he thought. If I stare at it, nothing will ever happen.

He began to pace once more and refrained from going to the beach, not wishing to relinquish his vantage point to observe the precise moment when the indicator would illuminate, signifying acceptance or rejection. He looked at the clock; it was now 4:01 p.m.

Time is slipping away, he thought.

At this rate, the week would be done in no time. Suddenly, his eyes sensed something new. He glanced over at the keyboard once more to see a red glow. On the computer screen was an error message and the word SP. He immediately searched for the codebook and fumbled through it, as his finger ran down the column of abbreviations. When he came upon the letters SP, he read the explanation on the right side of the page.

"Spelling error, it can't be!" he blurted, followed by several profanities.

It was the first time he had encountered this contingency and suddenly realized that there was no way to know precisely where he had made the error. There was only the page number as reference. In anger, he stormed outside to walk it off. He hadn't bothered to ask Chelston what he could do to locate the source of any mistake. But the professor had made it clear that he was not to contact him except in an emergency and this hardly qualified. Why hadn't he thought of this last night when he had him on the phone? Although Chelston said to keep him appraised, Schatten knew that this meant when Karamov responded.

He went in the house, turned on the computer and looked at the story as it appeared on the laptop. Painstakingly, he reviewed every line, hoping that he would find an obvious mistake that he had previously overlooked before blatantly entering the same mistake into the typewriter. But such was not the case. He knew that the word processor wasn't infallible and that spelling errors sometimes were missed by the program. Schatten poured over the page identified and then the entire submission over and over for an hour and a half but found nothing. His only alternative was to retype everything and pay particular attention to spelling.

He sat down in front of the old keyboard and carefully typed in the story once more. Two hours and fifteen minutes later, he submitted it again and resumed his pacing, like a caged tiger. Every excruciating minute passed with no response, no signal that the computer had made its decision. He was at his limit and couldn't handle another rejection for some petty error.

An hour passed before he opted for a glass of juice. As he finished his second drink, he again glanced over at the typewriter, and there to his elation was a glowing green light. At last, he had his first indication of the processing speed of the intricate system. Now it was only a matter to see how long it would take his adversary to respond if he would respond at all. His mind began to race with what if scenarios. He began to think, what if the Russian was merely trying to modify his work irrespective of what Schatten had written? But he soon dowsed this concept when he recalled that, after looking at the Russian's new material and comparing it to his own text, it was obvious that the man was targeting the changes. He also noted that Karamov didn't retype and resubmit the massive body of the work, but only those pages that Schatten had issued. Schatten had to assume that the body of the work was still stored inside the massive computer and that it wasn't necessary for the Russian to resubmit it before week's end. Karamov merely put a statement at the end of his text to reinstate the deletions that Schatten had made while also substituting new text to replace those sections that had been altered. He was beginning to get a better perspective of how the overall system functioned and what tricks each writer could employ.

Emotionally spent, Schatten decided to go outdoors and take a walk, but then he thought of remaining until his printer received Karamov's response. But as he began to reconsider, realizing that it could be hours before any activity occurred, a thought raced through his mind. The time of each transmission received would be kept as a record in the computer, and so he should be able to go back and see when the unit received the Russian's previous response. Schatten went to the screen and looked for the timeline as to when Karamov's changes were received and noted the time of 3:17 a.m. That was almost four hours from the time he sent his text until the moment when his printer activated. At least now he could rest assured that he wouldn't miss anything by leaving, for the time of any receipt of the Russian's response would be captured. Everything having to do with time was becoming an obsession with Schatten. He was beginning to feel pressed to respond as quickly as possible. It wasn't logical, but he was paranoid about the speed of this chess match.

Schatten decided to get out and relax for a change and savor the surroundings. He looked at his watch and changed into his swimsuit. Schatten went out to feel the sun on his face and the warm breeze blowing in, and he listened intently to the glorious sounds of the surf. He ran for about a quarter mile before impulsively plunging into the waves. Swimming out a way, he floated atop the gentle surf that began to carry him back to shore. The clear water wasn't very deep and barely rose above his waist. He stood and watched the small fishes scurry over the sandy bottom and around his feet. A large wave would roll in periodically and cause him to lose his balance. He marveled at the power of the ocean as it made him feel insignificant, and he liked that sensation. It served as a reminder that some things never changed and were dependable as well as timeless. Schatten again looked at his watch and noted that almost two hours had passed as the sun began to set. Feeling invigorated, he went back to the house to have a bowl of cereal. Entering the living room, he immediately looked over at the printer and saw no sign of activity. While eating his corn flakes, Schatten began to think about Karamov's responsiveness to his first alteration of the story. But the answer to the biggest nagging question that Schatten would never know was how quickly did the Russian receive the changes to his script? That was a major issue, for if Karamov received them immediately, he would not have to rush, having plenty of time to rewrite. When another hour went by without anything happening, Schatten was getting nervous. Three days were about to elapse, and he wanted to know immediately whether the Russian would respond.

Then he had a terrible thought, what if the Russian held back his response? This tactic would limit Schatten's ability to act. If his opponent waited until the last moment to counter, it would be virtually impossible to defeat the changes. He hoped that this would not be the case. But then he thought that if Karamov did respond within the same window that he had previously, he could employ this new strategy of delaying his rebuttal to the last possible moment so that it would come down to the wire.

Schatten could hold his cards in this poker game until the last possible moment, making it inconceivable for Karamov to respond in the time remaining. He only prayed that the Russian hadn't conceived of the same tactic. Schatten now understood that whoever responded last would be the victor, assuming he had time to be approved. The risk of waiting was that the submitter had to be accurate. There would be no room for error, for any mistake would mean disaster.

He decided to turn on the TV and wait for the printer to activate before he went anywhere. Then, looking at the time, he noted that it was 8:27 p.m. as the clock, like the raven in Poe's story, seemed to be tormenting him. Hours passed as he spent the time alternately pacing, watching TV, and walking the beach, but always never straying far from the printer. He finally sat down and began to organize other ways to defeat the plot and read more of the original story along with the Russian's latest insertions. Then he reclined on the couch and fell asleep. He awoke four hours later and looked over at the printer. His ear had been tuned to its distinctive sound, and he thought that it would have awakened him, had it activated. Schatten felt terrible, as though he hadn't slept at all. His senses were on edge and heightened, causing him to wake frequently from the slightest sound. He slowly got to his feet and walked over to the printer, searched, but saw nothing, as if it were capable of hiding sheets from him.

"Maybe I won," he said, as though saying it aloud would make it come true.

It was now several hours past the timeline that Schatten noted for the Russian's previous retort. His deepest fear now was that his adversary would wait until the last possible moment to reply to the latest changes. Every minute now was torturous, and he longed for the machine to come alive. Ironically, the absence of any response had now become the terrifying part. All Schatten needed was one more response from Karamov's to go on the offensive once more and hold the death blow to the entire plot until the last possible moment. But until then, the anticipation and the waiting were horrible.

14

A CHANGE IN THE WIND

IT WAS 2:38 A.M., AND HE COULDN'T SLEEP. He turned on the light and went over the Russian's story, looking for more areas to exploit, still waiting in silence. This was the beginning of the fourth day, and nothing had transpired. If the status quo continued, he would be the victor, but even if the Russian did respond, Schatten would take a new tack and attack his characters. Making any one or several of them fail would be just as effective to sabotage the storyline. The distasteful and unsavory nature of most of the group described would make it a simple matter to turn one of them into a traitor for the right price. After all, every one of them was a mercenary, and money was the motivating factor. But power was also a coveted commodity, and these two vices were highly sought. Any one of the cutthroats would sell out the other to obtain more. He studied every one of Karamov's creations and made detailed annotations on each. He compiled a file and made notes to clearly delineate the most acute weakness of every individual. Hours passed as Schatten wrote his biographies and the terrible things that each of his selected time bombs would do to shatter the plot.

The Arab fanatics were obvious targets. He wrote that von Weir's true sentiments for them and their cause would be discovered. This occurred when a mysterious tape appeared, capturing the leader's inner most thoughts during a conversation with his right-hand man, Ian Androkov. It would be a simple matter for the likes of Mohammad Izobyer, the leader of the Arab faction in Karamov's story, to listen to von Weir's hate spew from the recording. He would then realize that the leader was no different than any other Western infidel. He would organize a revolt within the ranks and try to enlist the others to follow. The Arab would then attack von Weir's supporters and seize the power and prestige for himself. If that failed, he would blow the whistle on the entire operation. He would receive a tidy sum for his trouble and go unscathed as all accountability and attention fell upon on von Weir.

Two more days passed without the printer's activation, and it was now the morning of the seventh and final day. If nothing was apparent by midnight, Schatten could declare victory and go on with his life. The world would never know of the theatrics in which he had been involved and how he had saved humanity. But he would have the solace that he did and in doing so had bested an author of extreme stature. His nerves were becoming frayed from lack of sleep as he entered the last lap of the race. His latest submission had been accepted by the SAM, but there was no response from the Russian. Schatten envisioned that his latest counter involving insurrection in the ranks would thwart Karamov. But the Russian had not responded, and his confidence was steadily eroding with every tick of the clock. Deep down, Schatten was becoming a basket case, but he was savvy enough to have written other counterplots as backups that were readily available, if required. But this assumed that Karamov would stay the course and not add some new twist.

The waiting was intolerable, and so Schatten continued to write. Since the printer had gone silent, he used his sleep time to pound away at the computer keyboard or to reread the Russian's work. Schatten tried to bolster his strained ego with the false bravado that his latest text would undermine anything that the Russian could bring to the table. But he was up against a highly unpredictable adversary in Karamov, and he sensed that something was about to transpire. On several occasions, he considered calling Chelston for advice but hesitated.

Schatten knew that the man would only offer encouragement and express additional surprise that the Russian could do what he previously had said was impossible. It was almost a pride issue now and begging for Chelston's help was the coward's way out. No, he was independent now and braced for another onslaught from Karamov.

Schatten put some frozen waffles into the toaster and fried some bacon as the sun rose signaling the final hours of the battle. He washed it all down with a glass of cranberry juice and then left to run down the beach. The early morning sun was warm, and scores of gulls and sandpipers were out fluttering about or scurrying across the sand for their breakfasts. Pelicans glided effortlessly before diving into the waves for their meals. His senses were alive as he waded into the cool water with his eyes taking on the great spectacle of the Atlantic Ocean. As he walked through the shallow water, an occasional large wave would act as a reminder of the sea's unpredictability. It was a further reminder that Karamov was the same way, and he could ill afford to take either for granted. His sleep deprivation almost provided him with a certain degree of euphoria, but his eyes were becoming heavy, and his mind was slowing along with his reflexes. He took off his shirt and heaved it up on the sand away from the surf. Schatten was now consumed with his surroundings and surrendered all his feelings to it. Walking further out, he plunged into the water. Opening his eyes, he saw dozens of tiny fish swim rhythmically with the current and saw the presence of many shells dotting the sand beneath the waves. For the first time since the entire gut-wrenching experience began, he felt free. He rose to his feet and put his hands over his eyes to try and remove the saltwater's sting. Looking toward the horizon, he noted the huge mountains of clouds blowing out to the ocean and saw dolphins leap from the surface and then plunge back, puncturing the tranquility of the glistening green sea.

Then the thought of the printer suddenly crept back into his mind as a dose of reality tore through him like a cold wind. He was inexplicably guilt ridden over the pure joy he was experiencing while savoring his surroundings. It was as though it was a decadent luxury, he could ill afford until the ordeal had played itself out. He retrieved his shirt and slowly trudged back to see if the Russian had provided anything new. When he opened the door, his eyes immediately fixed upon the printer. It stood idle, and the sound of its silence was almost unbearable. He took a shower and let the warm water envelop him for several minutes. Then he dressed and sat down at the table and reviewed all the folders that he had amassed over the last few days. They contained his notes on characters and perceived weaknesses in the Russian's plot that he could exploit. He decided to press on and assure that everything was polished as his fingers played a literary symphony on the computer's keyboard. Drug addiction and alcoholism were added to the mix as additional vices and sources of weakness for various characters. Then he looked over the Russian's text and marked up the pages of the current plot where each new detail would be added. Schatten was hopeful that when he injected these new sordid character embellishments into the plot, they would stand up to the scrutiny of the soulless arbiter and critic—the SAM computer.

The clock was always there as each second ticked toward the finish line, and it was now 12:02 p.m., and he was stymied as there was nothing that he could do. Like it or not, he had lost control over the situation. But he couldn't dwell upon it, for it would only eat him up inside, more than it already had. Then he thought of breaking the tension by going into town and having lunch. He grabbed his wallet and headed out and took his time. He observed all the scenic vistas afforded to him as part of the winding state highway that led to the sleepy little New England village. He decided to go to the little diner where everything had begun. He consumed his meal and got back into his car. He passed the liquor store and decided to buy a bottle of Champagne for his upcoming victory celebration at midnight. This gave him added courage and provided a symbol of victory if he was patient and survived the last painful hours.

He returned to the beach house at 3:46 p.m. and immediately checked the printer, but there was nothing. Schatten did denote that the light on the typewriter that had previously signified his rejection and subsequent approval of his submissions was unlit once more. He continued to organize the Russian's work and read through some areas that he hadn't previously seen. Then he turned on the TV and watched the Red Sox/Yankee game.

The hours slipped away, and before he knew what was happening, it was 8:51 p.m., and he had drifted off into a semi-dream state due to his exhaustion. But he hadn't really slept, so Schatten went to the kitchen sink and threw a handful of cold water on his face and knew that he must stay sharp.

He went over to the table and picked up another file, going over more of Karamov's story when the computer started printing at a furious pace. His heart sank to the floor, having resigned himself to the fact that the Russian had surrendered or at least wasn't privy to his last submission. Unabated, the pages began to fill the tray before spilling out on the floor as a paralyzed Schatten stood in abject fear watching the reams of text come through. The war had rekindled. He was shaking as he picked up the latest text and began to browse through everything being received. Seconds turned to minutes as he began to try and organize all that was being hurled at him. He finally got control of his emotions and began to coolly get to the heart of the submission. New characters were evident, and an entirely new plot was beginning to unfold.

There had been a change in the wind, an alteration of tactics. It was something that he'd sensed for days, sitting in the back of his mind like a weird, gnawing premonition. Nearly an hour had soon gone by with no let up, as though this was the final assault of the last battle. Schatten had to survive this now, but when would it end? It then stopped, mercifully, as Schatten picked up the last pages. He sorted through, looking to find the ending, but found none. Then it became painfully apparent that something was wrong. Suddenly, the computer and the printer indicated that an ink cartridge required replacement.

He fumbled through the instructions and replaced the expended cartridges. Then the procession of printing continued for a few minutes and abruptly stopped, and he exhaled with a sigh of relief. To his horror, he noted that the printer was merely out of paper. Schatten reloaded it, and the volume continued, unrestrained. He couldn't afford to panic now, he had to use the same skill he had acquired on the previous submittal and not get wrapped up in the volume of Karamov's latest offering and simply concentrate on the details.

At 10:01 p.m., the printer halted its production. He began organizing at a furious pace. All the characters were new, other than von Weir and Androkov. The plot now involved a series of suitcase bombs and biological agents. There was no mention of the submarine or the storming of the ICBM complex. Instead, the Arab fanatics would be sent out in great numbers worldwide to place small nuclear devices in thirty-six major cities. This would be accompanied by the dispensing of a horrendous biological creation of unmatched lethality, which would also be placed at strategic locations to eliminate huge numbers of the world's military and civilian populous.

The virus was airborne and would be released by aerosol cans. Von Weir alone would control the antidote and have every nation groveling at his feet for it. Schatten began to compose himself and sat down to list every character that Karamov had created in the new scenario. Schatten thought that the best way to defeat the plot was to adapt what he had already written to these new players.

But his descriptions were so tied to the old characters that he would have to rewrite almost every detail. He had paid the price for trying to copy the Russian's style for accuracy, instead of being more generic.

Midnight continued to loom over him. Every second counted; he had no time to waste.

He thought that it might be easier to find the weaknesses in the new lethal devices that the Russian was about to employ. Thus said, he had to go into the secret database once more and immediately learn everything he could.

He looked at the clock, now looking more and more like a vulture, and saw that it was 10:14 p.m. Schatten went through the series of passwords and again entered the eerie realm of the most secret. He immediately searched for portable nuclear devices. Several terms now emblazoned the screen, one of which was the phrase "suitcase bomb." He then remembered that he had seen this phrase in the new text. Clicking on this term, Schatten was now privy to a page devoted to a series of lethal weapons small enough to be stowed inside a backpack. Some created by the US in the 1970s were small enough to actually fit inside a small suitcase. The yield of such a device was about one kiloton. Since the bombs dropped on Japan at the later stages of World War II delivered an explosive yield of sixteen kilotons of explosives, these devices introduced by Karamov seemed meager by comparison. But just to make sure, Schatten grabbed the stack of pages from the Russian's latest text and nervously scanned down page after page until he found the details of the small nuclear devices. The Russian told in extensive detail how von Weir had paid a fortune to several disgruntled scientists to miniaturize these types of weapons, even further, while increasing their explosive power by fourfold. He searched through the data to see if he could find any mention of such developments and found one paragraph that told of Russian attempts to accomplish exactly what Karamov was suggesting. Now he knew that it was plausible, and so he searched for a weakness in the device. He found schematics of both the Russian and US designs. He typed in failure mode into the search window on the upper right-hand side of the screen. In a moment, it showed the flaws in both systems. Apparently, the trigger mechanisms were problematic. Static electricity was an issue with these weapons as demonstrated by a fateful detonation in a Russian research laboratory. The trigger had to be insulated to prevent any reoccurrence of this event, and both sides became acutely aware of this problem. Ceramic materials were used in lieu of metal, but the mechanism broke frequently. Composite materials were tried, but the reliability was still extremely low. When metal was tried once more, with the addition of extreme amounts of insulation, the results were better, but the metal corroded which led to other issues. Schatten furiously made renderings of both schematics along with notes on every flaw of the devices. Then he went back quickly to see if he had missed anything in the Russian's description and was satisfied that he had not.

He was about to search for the biological weapons section when the alarm went off, causing him to almost jump out of his seat.

It was 11:02, and he had only ten minutes left to find the data and then only 48 minutes to defeat the plot.

Schatten poured through the computer screen, looking for anything on bioweapons. Engaging the search mode once more, he was soon staring at a page full of toxins, none of which he could pronounce. Then, rummaging through Karamov's story, he found the pages devoted to the bioweapons. It was an airborne virus that needed only to contact the skin or inhaled to kill instantly. He frantically looked for its name in the list of offerings but couldn't find it. Schatten then nervously typed the name directly into the search window, and the screen then displayed what he sought.

Then he looked at the clock, he had two minutes. He furiously began to scribble notes on what could stem the virus. Apparently, there were recognized antidotes, and he copied their names.

He looked at the clock once more and saw that he was now one minute past his allotted safe time. He was in the danger zone, but he couldn't turn back now. He had to have the data to foil the last portion of the plot. Schatten went at breakneck speed, writing down every detail of the bioweapon and how it could be dispensed and how it attacked the nervous system.

He was almost done, but it was now 11:22. Suddenly, the phone rang and kept ringing until he answered it.

"Michael, what are you doing? You've overstayed your welcome, boy; get out of the database now! Do you hear me, Michael? They know where you are; you have to get out, now! Pack up everything and take it with you. Take everything and get out, now!" yelled a furious Chelston.

"But I have to respond. I can't leave now!" shouted Schatten.

"Michael, don't argue, just leave or they will be there and arrest you. Do you understand? It's over. Leave now!"

15
ZERO HOUR

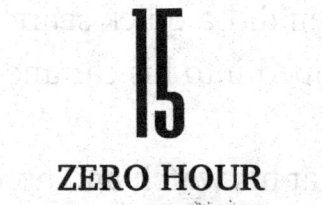

THE SPECTER OF MIDNIGHT LOOMED even closer, and he couldn't afford the luxury of burning even a second. But now, he was sidetracked and had to overcome being found and arrested. Schatten grabbed the typewriter, rushed to his car, and opened the trunk. He ran back and carried out the computer and printer before going back again for the monitor. Then he amassed all the paper and stuffed it into the trunk. Schatten did a quick search of the room before he jumped into his car and sped off into the night.

He looked at his watch and noted that it was 11:32 p.m.

His mind was racing as fast as his heart.

Schatten remembered a place up the highway that just might have vacancies; at least he prayed they would. Increasing his speed, he looked desperately for the motel sign. The minutes were ticking away now, and every one of them that went by brought him one step closer to defeat and the end of the world at midnight. Suddenly, his eyes caught a glimpse of a red glow, and he knew immediately that it was the hotel.

His heart was pounding so loud that he thought that it would leave his chest. He pulled into the driveway and ran to the office. There was no one at the desk, so he pounded on the bell continuously. Then, a little old, balding man sporting a gray beard that matched his thinning hair and bushy eyebrows emerged from the back room.

"Yes, yes," he said, perturbed by the disturbance. "Young people are always in a hurry."

"Yes, I am, and I need a room," barked Schatten.

He looked at his watch. It was 11:45 p.m.

"Well you're in luck, young fella. Just happen to have a couple. Now this one overlooks the lake and has a great view," responded the proprietor.

Schatten, nervously looking at his watch, replied, "That'll be fine, how much for one night?"

"Eighty-seven fifty-six with tax," said the old gentleman, in the same thick New England brogue as the shopkeeper.

Schatten fumbled through his wallet and pulled out two fifty-dollar bills and said, "Keep the change," as he turned to sprint out the door.

"Not so fast, young fella," said the manager. "There's also a fifty-dollar deposit that you get back when you leave."

"Here," snapped Schatten as he plucked another fifty from his wallet.

Schatten didn't have time for any conversations, and his patience was running low. He just wanted to get inside a room, any room, to try and pound out something in the time remaining. Fraught with emotion and not thinking clearly, he slammed open the door and stood outside for a few seconds. It suddenly dawned on him that he didn't know where the room was, nor did he have a key. Now even more angered by his own stupidity, he barged through the door once more, only to see the proprietor staring at him and smirking.

"I think you'll need this," he said, dangling the key on the end of his index finger. "Now take the road that runs by the office all the way to the right about a quarter mile, and you'll see cabin fifteen on the left."

"Thanks," said Schatten, as he snatched the key from the man's hand and barreled out the door.

Schatten jumped behind the wheel of his car and slammed the door. The tires threw gravel in every direction as Schatten sped to the small cabin. He found it without any issue and drove up as close as he could but at too high a speed, forcing him to slam on the brakes. Schatten flung open the door, leapt from the driver's seat, slammed the door shut, and sprinted to open the trunk. He ran to the door of the cabin, unlocked it, and scanned the darkened room, only barely illuminated by the porch light. He hurriedly walked inside, found a floor lamp, and turned it on. The screen door had no mechanism to lock it in the open position, and he struggled to get through it. He used his foot to keep it open as both arms were occupied carrying the computer hardware and the typewriter. He nervously looked at his watch and saw that it was 11:52 p.m.

"You can do this, come on, Schatten," he muttered, with teeth clenched.

He realized that he would have no time to plug in the computer and would have to type his story directly into the typewriter. He took a deep breath and sat in front of the keyboard as his mind began to compose his submittal. There was no room for error now, and he had to be exact. He looked for the Russian's pages that he had just scanned to find where he would input his composition.

Every second that ticked off the clock was now magnified, and he kept one eye on the time as though this action could slow it down. He fumbled through his adversary's work until he found the pages that he had marked less than an hour before. Schatten quickly began to write his story to mesh with Karamov's.

It was 11:54 p.m.

Without wasting a minute more, he sat in front of the typing machine and began entering his composition. He wrote: "All the suitcase bombs had an inherent flaw, as their trigger mechanisms were not only brittle but subject to jamming. When the devices were smuggled into the respective countries, none functioned. They were cheap metal stampings to reduce costs, and each was an exact duplicate of the others with the same discrepancy. The prototype had been handcrafted, but the production versions had not received the same level of attention to detail. The Arab terrorists who were to act as von Weir's cannon fodder and trigger the devices as suicidal acts in support of their Jihad were now disgraced. They went on rampages, wielding hand weapons and knives to take down as many infidels as they could to at least save their dignity. Grabbing hostages indiscriminately, they planned to go on a mass killing spree but were immediately captured and interrogated as one of the assassins disclosed the entire plot. Flaws in the canisters containing the biological weapons also failed to function due to faulty valves. When this occurred, these individuals also tried to take the same tactic to slaughter as many people as they could as a measure of retribution for the failure. All were unable to dispense the biological weapons and were apprehended before they could accomplish any bedlam."

Then Schatten added that von Weir was captured, tried, and executed, and Schatten instructed the computer to delete everything after page 86. This was the cutoff point where Karamov told of the mass worldwide hysteria and devastation resulting from the actions of his fanatic minions. He then nervously hit the send button and glanced at his watch. It was 11:58 p.m.

"I did it! I made it!" he shouted in jubilation as his knees buckled and he dropped to the floor.

The entire weight of what he had been through cascaded through his body like a bolt of lightning. He sank to the floor as his emotions gave way, and tears began to stream down his face.

"If only I'd brought that Champagne with me," he said laughing.

His joy knew no bounds as his emotions soared. Schatten got to his knees and pumped his fists into the air and leaped as high as he could. Elation, unlike anything he had experienced, permeated through his entire being and into his very soul. He was filled with a sense of accomplishment and pride in the fact that he had overcome adversity. He placed his hands over his face; he was in a euphoric freefall. It was the Indianapolis Colts winning the Super bowl; it was getting a set of those wonderful steel Tonka Trucks for Christmas morning when he was ten.

Then he glanced at the typewriter and saw the red glow.

It was as if someone had drained the oxygen from the room and punched him in the stomach. From euphoria to manic depression in under five seconds.

"What?" he screamed. "It can't be, it was perfect."

He nervously plugged in the computer to see the accompanying code. Schatten couldn't wait for the machine to boot up and began to shout at it. When the screen finally showed the rejection in graphic terms the code PS stood out. Schatten angrily sifted through the codebook until he found the PS definition. It read, "Partial Submission."

"What does that mean, partial submission?" he shouted angrily.

The small book deciphered that the term meant that the plot had not been fully altered and so had been rejected.

A seething Schatten began to look through all the Russian's work. He found that he hadn't even seen the other sections of the latest text since he had been so absorbed by the new characters and weaponry. But this was only a ruse as the Russian had also put an abbreviated version of the previous plot behind this new storyline. The capturing of the submarine and the ICBM complex were still there but rewritten to render Schatten's previous changes moot. Karamov had gambled that Schatten would be so entrenched at solving the problem of his new additions that he would fail to realize that the Russian had resubmitted the old plot as well, with new modifications. Schatten had been duped and outmaneuvered by his opponent.

His head felt like it was in a vice. It was too much to contemplate. He had lost to the master. When it became clear that Karamov had masterfully executed a diversion, Schatten looked at the final page of Karamov's last submittal.

There, at the bottom of the page below the word END, was the word **CHECKMATE** in bold letters. Apparently, the Russian knew that this was the coup de grâce. Zero hour, midnight, had passed, and it was all over; Schatten had come up short. It was so bitter a defeat that he was unable to cope with it. He stared at the clock as though it could rewind. If only he had read further and knew what the Russian had up his sleeve. Deception was a component of war, and Schatten was now schooled. He had failed not only himself, but all of humanity.

16
DRASTIC ACTION

THE WITCHING HOUR HAD COME AND gone, leaving Schatten alone with his thoughts, and the problem remained unsolved. The celebratory atmosphere had become a funeral procession for a dead mission. The wall clock seemed to grow in size, and it read 12:13 a.m. Elation, shock, and disbelief had given way to a new set of emotions. Within this normally rational individual, now festered a gaping, open wound. He became a caldron into which was poured a simmering mass of frustration, self-loathing, guilt, depression, and unbridled anger. It now boiled over into an inferno of hatred for the man who had caused his plight. He now viewed the Russian as no more than vermin or a disease. Schatten could not allow the entire world to be dragged into Karamov's sordid view of reality. He had one obsession now—rectifying his mistakes by exorcising the demon responsible. It was the middle of the night, but it was impossible for him to sleep. He was running on adrenaline and simply felt numb. Now, his only goal was to fly to London and somehow find and face his nemesis.

It would take him several hours to drive to Boston's Logan Airport, and he had no inkling of the time of the earliest flight. The shroud of defeat enveloped his very soul as he checked out of the hotel and retrieved his deposit.

After loading all his equipment into the trunk, he sat for a moment in his car, head pressed against the steering wheel. He was a failure in every respect and had disgraced himself. There was no miracle answer; he had simply failed. The euphoria of piecing together the final part of the puzzle and the glory of outwitting the adversary and cheating the devil from his due were not realized. Instead, rejection, self-doubt, a feeling of ineptness, coupled with remorse filled every ounce of his being.

Worst of all, the anticipation of impending doom crept into his very soul. How could he have possibly summoned the genius to save the world? As though Atlas buckled under duress from the weight of the earth, he had crumbled under the pressure of undoing plot after insidious plot. Don Quixote, armed with his typewriter instead of a lance, failed to slay the dragon now loosed upon an unsuspecting world. But beyond his personal introspection and analysis of how the entire ordeal had become the ultimate failure, there was one overriding emotion that now consumed him and displaced all others.

Rage had supplanted all, and blind vengeance displaced self-recrimination. What survived in the emotional aftermath of failure was the clear-cut directive to remove the cancer. There was only one alternative now—he must cut off the head of the snake. How could anything remain of the plot if the author was eliminated? The plan was simple, he would wait until the airport opened, fly to London, then take the train to Salisbury, locate Karamov, and somehow summon the nerve to kill him.

He raced to Boston Logan Airport, where he parked his car into the first space that he saw. Then, inexplicably, his mind was overwhelmed by an incredible idea. Schatten leaped out of the car and recovered the typewriter from the trunk. Sitting in the passenger seat, he began typing furiously while the thoughts were still fresh in his head.

He finished, hit the send button, and then placed the unit back in the trunk. Schatten briefly considered carrying the typewriter on the plane but reasoned that it would never make it past security. But he was fortunate that he had gathered all his identification, including his passport, before he was unceremoniously ejected from the secret database and his cottage.

He dared not go back to the place since he faced the real possibility that he could run into federal agents who may want to take him into custody.

He sprinted to the terminal, selected a flight from several airline schedules, and stood in line for his ticket. Schatten passed the time walking through the terminal, waiting for the 7 p.m. flight, which was the only one available. He hadn't brought his clothes or suitcase from the beach house, having left so abruptly. This required that he purchase a duffel bag, sweat suit, and two days' worth of clothes on the way. Hours later, Schatten boarded the plane and took his window seat in the last row.

As the doors closed, Schatten likened it to the lid of his coffin being nailed shut, and he suddenly felt as if he would not return. He stared at the pulsating, flashing red collision light on the tip of the long, majestic left wing. It was almost hypnotic and mirrored his heartbeat as he thought of the consequences of letting Karamov get away with it. Then he measured this against the terrible thought of taking a human life. As the plane sailed into the star-laden sky and darkness covered the aircraft some hours later, several scenarios rang through his head. The aircraft left the North American continent and headed for the open North Atlantic. Now, he had ample time to ponder how he would handle the situation if and when he confronted the man.

As the hours passed and the darkness abated, the sun illuminated his watch at midnight. He closed his shade and tried to sleep, but to no avail. The aircraft soared into the new day in the English time zone, and the passengers were now being awakened as the cabin lights were turned on. He disdained the food and beverage offerings from the flight attendant in an effort to concentrate solely on the task ahead now that the plane was only an hour from London. Was there anything that Karamov could offer that would dissuade him, or had it gone too far? Was the only answer a swift strike of retribution, atoning for his failings and saving the millions affected across the face of the Earth by this mad man? Hadn't the world seen enough of Hitler, Stalin, and other assorted megalomaniacs?

Then he looked down to see the unmistakable beauty of the English countryside, resplendent in all its distinctive multihued greenery, most notably, the hedgerows and clusters of trees. Once the plane landed at Gatwick Airport, he made the arduous trek through customs and then proceeded to the train terminal within the complex and bought a ticket for Salisbury. He anxiously awaited the first train's arrival, but it was late, and he paced up and down the concrete platform in anticipation. The flashing schedules affixed to the underside of the platform's overhanging roof provided an up-to-date listing of each approaching train. When it finally arrived, he found a seat next to the window easily enough and placed his bag on his lap on the first leg of the route through Clapham Junction.

This was one of the bustling terminals on the outskirts of London. There, numerous connections are made with the rail services for all of England. As the car ambled along, he noticed the overhead, aluminum luggage racks, sloping upward with barely enough room to sustain a normal briefcase. The car wheels clanked in that rhythmic symphony that only trains can produce. Occasionally, the pattern was broken by a swift moving express, traveling in the opposite direction that shot by unexpectedly, producing a rush of wind along with a pronounced whistling sound. The noise level of its clattering wheels intensified in direct proportion to its speed as it disappeared as quickly as it had made its presence known. Arriving at the station, he was totally confused regarding which train departed to Salisbury. He grew impatient trying to read the schedules posted on the large boards, and so asked one of the conductors for guidance.

He was instructed to proceed to platform twelve, where the train would arrive in short order. Schatten thanked the man and then rushed up several tiers of steps. Guided by a series of signs painted upon the brick walls, he found the platform with the train awaiting departure. He boarded quickly and had a car to himself, placing his bag in one of the larger luggage racks in the rear. The trip would take almost two hours, allowing him to reflect coldly and calmly on every action required to accomplish the mission in true military fashion.

First, could he purchase a weapon? The sale of a gun seemed impossible in a country that controlled firearms so rigidly, and in addition, he was a foreigner. He would play it by ear and use anything at his disposal when he entered the house. The first order of business was to find the residence and reconnoiter the surroundings. He left the train at the picturesque little station at Salisbury and walked the mile distance to the center of town. Schatten found a map of the surroundings at a local hotel. He asked the woman at the front desk and several people staying at the facility if they knew where the Karamov residence was located but to no avail. Visiting the local library, he used the Internet to locate the man. He gauged the distance between he and the home of his intended victim using one of the website's features.

It gave a detailed route from the hotel where he had booked a room for the night to Karamov's. It was four miles to Karamov's residence, and he decided to walk the route as a practice run to the actual event. He passed by rows of quaint little shops and restaurants with the brick fronts painted in a variety of pastels before coming to a park. He checked his map and continued his excursion to the outskirts of town. Schatten walked precariously on the narrow curb, as there was no sidewalk, as is typical of the English countryside.

Finally having traversed the 4.1 miles, he came upon a stately manor replete with an iron gate, high brick wall, and protective fence. There would be no easy way in, and climbing the wall was the only alternative. Schatten tried not to look suspicious while taking several photos, in typical tourist fashion, with his digital camera. He observed the doors and windows to surmise which offered the easiest possible entry. Then he walked back to the hotel after stopping in a small shop, offering Cornish pasties and sausage rolls for a light lunch. Then he worked the plan out in his mind, going over various scenarios and escapes. He purchased a glasscutter, thirty feet of sturdy rope, a pair of work gloves, clay, a flashlight, and batteries at the local hardware store and a backpack from another shop. Then he whiled away the hours and walked around town in the area surrounding the main park before settling on a bench overlooking St. Catherine's Cathedral. He looked skyward at the mammoth stone structure, under renovation. Trying to collect his thoughts, he sat marveling at its architecture, replete with flying buttresses and numerous sculptures carved on its walls. Lost in thought, he continuously checked his watch as the sun was beginning to set as it approached 9 p.m., and he elected to go back to the hotel for last-minute preparations. This was a night operation, and so he had to wait for darkness to fall.

Before Schatten returned to his hotel, he purchased a black sweat suit, which he donned shortly after entering his room, along with his trusty old running shoes. He placed the glasscutter, gloves, clay, flashlight, and thirty feet of rope in his backpack. Lying on the bed, he reviewed every digital picture he had taken of the house. He watched TV periodically until darkness had fallen, when he decided to start his trek. Schatten made a series of notes that he could check off when he reached Karamov's property. He was clearly out of his league and comfort zone on this venture but reasoned that following a systematic checklist just might serve as the deterrent to panicking and aborting the mission.

But obtaining a weapon was still unfinished business. Perhaps he would find an instrument at the home of the author. His mind was racing now, and he was so nervous that he was shaking as the plan played out over and over in his head. Schatten would station himself by the wall on the right side of the dwelling where a large tree provided a degree of cover. Scaling the wall, he would lower himself with the rope that would also serve for his escape.

Next, he would use the glasscutter to make a hole in the window to access the latch and gain entree. Then, he would enter and lie in wait, then terminate, by whatever means, the author who threatened to deliver the antichrist to the pinnacle of power. But if no one appeared, he would search the house until he found the typewriter and return it to Chelston. Then he thought that even if he discovered the other typewriter, he could never get it through customs with the heightened security stemming from 9/11. But he would figure that one out later.

12

CABBAGES AND KINGS

HE WALKED BRISKLY ALONG THE STEEP roadside leading from Salisbury until finally coming upon the house and its formidable wall. He surveyed the entire perimeter, looking for a place to anchor the rope and scale the wall. Then remembering his notes, he quickly retrieved them from the right pocket of his sweatpants. He carefully trained his flashlight on the pages and crouched down to ensure that the light was concealed. As he scanned his notes, he was suddenly reminded of the large tree to his right, some fifty feet away, and hurried over to it. Gauging the tree's position relative to the wall, he leaped up and caught the lowest branch. Dangling for a few moments, he summoned the strength to raise himself. He now rose to his feet, noting that he was in a good position to scale the next series of branches. Schatten continued to climb until he reached a large branch that was located just above the top of the wall. Easing his way onto the limb, he crawled out as far as he could. Then, he precariously contorted his frame to place himself in the position to leap atop the wall. Struggling to get into position, he thrust himself outward and landed ungracefully on the brick structure. Schatten clung on unstably before he righted himself, lacerating his left hand and knee in the process. Then, he maneuvered his feet over the edge and awkwardly dropped down to the ground below, forgetting to use the rope to aid in his escape. But it was too late now, and he scolded himself mentally for this bit of stupidity. This wasn't like James Bond films where everything was done so easily. He had bruised his body and hands in several places but disdained the pain and moved on, staying low. Now lying down on the grounds of his adversary, he quickly surveyed the driveway for vehicles and signs of movement inside the house. Seeing what appeared to be an empty dwelling, he then rushed to the side of the two-story, brick structure. Affixing the putty to a pane of glass, he cut a circle with his glasscutter into the window. He carefully removed the section and placed it at his feet, utilizing the putty as the handle. Reaching inside, he unlatched and then opened the window. His heart was racing as he entered. Finding himself in the study, he stopped to listen for anything that sounded like movement or a presence. Breathing heavily and sweating profusely, he hoped that no one could hear his heart pound. This wasn't fantasy, it was hard, dangerous reality. His mind was racing. He had just broken into a private residence of a very powerful man and could be shot as a trespasser. *What would be his defense should the police arrest him?* His story was so absurd that they would likely laugh in his face before throwing him into jail. *What about silent alarms or dogs or henchmen?*

It's a little late for that, you idiot, he thought. You should have thought of that before you let yourself in.

The house was dark with dim patches of light emanating from one or two lamps located in other adjacent rooms. He had entered into the drawing room and proceeded into a large sitting room. He carefully scanned the entire area and listened intently for any sound indicating that anyone else was there. He crept low, trying desperately to be silent. If anyone other than Karamov appeared, he would bolt for the window through which he had entered. His senses were in a heightened state of alert, and every sound, every shadow, became a potential threat. Ominous shadows were everywhere as his flashlight illuminated each corner of every room.

He fumbled for his notes and then began to search the house, looking for the man first and then the typewriter. But he required a weapon, and so he visited the kitchen and found a small but sturdy butcher's knife. He carefully placed it into the pocket of his jacket and slowly scoured the first floor from the dining area to the study. Every board that creaked sounded like a gunshot to his paranoid senses.

He now searched for the stairs and was relieved to find them in the next room. He then became aware of a pronounced rhythmic ticking and looked around to find a rather large grandfather clock attached to the wall to his immediate right. Then he began to climb the stairs, attempting to place as little pressure as possible on his feet to minimize the sound. As each board creaked, his heart sank, and his level of paranoia rose, if that was possible. As he continued to climb, he looked back periodically and then up the top of the staircase to see if anyone appeared. After what seemed like hours, he finally made it to the top and systematically began checking every room. Slowly walking down the hallway decorated with expensive artwork, he checked the first room to his left.

He carefully turned the knob and opened the door. Using his flashlight, he scanned the room for anything resembling the typewriter. His primary objective now was to capture the typewriter, thereby undoing everything without any retribution. This was wishful thinking and unsupported, but he felt instinctively that this was true. But if this failed, he would stick to the plan—killing Karamov. The thought made his stomach turn.

He went to the next room and entered slowly, again scanning every inch with his flashlight. Finding nothing, he moved on. Entering the third room, he noted that there was a large desk to his left and a high-backed chair. On the desk, in plain sight, was something that he held out little hope of seeing; it was the typewriter. Although he was overjoyed at the appearance of the unit, it really wasn't a total surprise. For before he ventured inside the Boston airport, he had hastily written the event on his typewriter in the car.

Knowing that he could not compose anything in which he would be directly involved, he merely wrote a scenario whereby Karamov's unit would be lying on the desk in an unlocked room. But he didn't know if Karamov had seen his story or even if his little vignette had been accepted by the main computer. As it turned out, it somehow had miraculously gotten through the gauntlet. Now the question was should he escape with the unit or destroy it? But how could he destroy it?

That wasn't an option now. Schatten couldn't help but dwell on the fact that through Karamov's device, the Russian had somehow changed the rules of the game. Now Karamov could flesh out a story where he was one of the lead characters. He could literally create the world in his image apparently.

But if such was the case, why destroy the world? He could not resist putting his hand upon the device that threatened the end of life as he knew it.

Schatten knew immediately when he laid his hands upon it that he could interface with the machine. In his composition, he had specified that this was Karamov's typewriter. He had recalled how he was able to interact with Prescott's boat, so he assumed it would work with Karamov's machine.

Then, inexplicably, a series of thoughts exploded into his mind just as they had at Logan Airport in Boston. He put down his flashlight and sat down before the typewriter. He began pressing the keys furiously, compelled to capture every thought that had rushed into his brain like a tidal wave. His mind, rife with clarity, now envisioned the path to solving everything in one swift stroke.

It was akin to his first introduction to his device when the words flowed from his mind and into the typewriter as though he was having an out of body experience. He felt the all-consuming power of the machine somehow control his mind, as though it was an extension of him. Then he stopped abruptly, as if awakened from a trance.

What am I doing? he thought. I've no time for this, grab the machine and run!

Suddenly as he came to his senses, he felt a tremendous pressure pulling his right arm behind his body. In the very same instant, his face was thrust into the desk top. Someone placed a knee into his back, then grabbed the hair on the back of his head and yanked upward. The individual then took Schatten's flashlight and shined the beam directly into his eyes. Next, he felt cold steel on the back of his neck and heard the cocking of the trigger.

"The time has come, the Walrus said, to talk of many things," said the voice, with a slight accent, quoting Lewis Carroll.

"If you move one inch, I insert two bullets right into your brain. Do we understand each other?" asked the voice.

Schatten was lifted to his feet and told to place his hands against the wall with feet spread, then frisked for any sign of a weapon. His attacker quickly found the knife and threw it across the room.

The assailant then thrust him back into the chair as, all the while, the light from the flashlight was blinding him.

"And who might you be, my friend?" asked the attacker.

Schatten did not reply which caused the barrel of the gun to be placed directly on his right temple.

"Now, I will ask again, and I suggest you answer. Who are you?"

"M-Michael Schatten," he responded nervously, his heart ready to jump out of his chest.

"Now, that's better. Alright, who is Michael Schatten, and why is he in my house?"

"I'm a writer," Schatten replied.

The gun was removed as his assailant moved away, but the light still shone in his eyes, making it impossible to see anything.

"I suppose you are an admirer of my work and hoped to gather a souvenir?"

"Ah-yes, that's it exactly," Schatten responded.

"Then what about the knife?" he shouted. "I hope your writing skills are better than your skills as an assassin. You know you are quite lucky that it was I who found you and not one of my security people. I just came back to gather up a few things before my trip."

"Where are you going?" asked Schatten.

"Oh, let's just say an extended holiday and leave it at that."

"South America, I presume?" asked Schatten.

"How did you know that?" Karamov asked in a curious tone.

"The missile base, the submarine, I know the whole plot," replied Schatten in frustration and fear.

"Wait a second—you're him, aren't you? Of course, you were the one writing the plots. Well, this does change things. One never tires of meeting the enemy face-to-face. Bravo, Mr. Schatten. You presented quite a challenge . . . for a few hours. Well done, my boy, I rather enjoyed it. I didn't think the old professor could pull it off. No hard feelings, I hope. By the way, it was never a level playing field, but I'll give you credit. I really think you have potential. Too bad all your efforts were moot."

Schatten was flabbergasted that Karamov could make the link between him and the counterplots so quickly.

"You know about the professor?" asked Schatten, shocked.

"I am FSB. I know everything. I assumed they were tracking me. When I saw your writing, it confirmed it. The Russians have tracked this project since the 1940s. I take it that you were part of his group?"

"No, I was recruited after I stumbled upon the typewriter in an antique store. I began to write my novel with it when its properties became apparent. I contacted the professor, and he enlisted me to undo your work," replied Schatten.

"I hope they paid you," said the Russian.

"Yes, they did. Let me ask you something?" said Schatten. "You altered the machine, right? How'd you do it?"

"I'm afraid I don't understand the question, my friend. Can you be more specific?" asked Karamov.

"I was told that the person operating the typewriter could never involve themselves in the storyline. I found that to be true. Apparently, you altered the protocols and did whatever you pleased. How did you alter the system?"

"You know, it gives me great pleasure to have this conversation. One wonders if anyone really appreciates true genius. Certainly, the good professor could never bring himself to do so. You know, I'm actually beginning to like you, and since you probably will never leave this house alive, I find it stimulating to tell all, as it were. Someone that's appreciative, that almost makes it all worthwhile. Where to begin? Well, I started out discovering the power of the unit. I can't say precisely when I realized how this simple device could change everything, but having the manual certainly helped. You see when I purchased the thing, it came with a user's manual, I suppose you Americans would say. It was very useful in the dos and don'ts but didn't cover the physics involved. Well, for that I used my KGB friends. You realize that we, the Russians, penetrated the development of the atomic bomb which your country named the Manhattan Project. Obviously, if we could do that, this project should have been simple by comparison. But that was far from the truth. This project, the development of the typewriters, had striking potential. Trying to penetrate the security surrounding the super computer posed a bigger problem to those gathering intelligence than any other project. My colleagues had abandoned their efforts without realizing the full scope of the scheme. Only I saw its full range of possibilities. So when I came upon the typewriter and the manual, I was elated to say the least. It's not often that such a windfall shows itself in one's lifetime. I knew the implications of this device, and I coveted its power. I was in no mood to share its capabilities with Mother Russia. No, I knew the stupidity of the average government bureaucrat and understood that it would be a disaster if some dimwitted party member tried to experiment with it. So, I carefully cultivated the scientists I needed to make the system function to suit my needs. I paid millions and lined the pockets of several top minds. You see, greed is a universal principal. I also knew that the Americans had dropped the ball; I think is the proper term? So I merely picked it up and finished the game," he said chuckling.

"So it wasn't you at all, it was your mercenaries who did the work," said Schatten.

"Now that was very unkind, in fact, insulting—but accurate," he said chuckling. "I hate to disappoint you that I am not a genius, but I am a visionary. It was at my direction." Karamov snapped.

"So, your ultimate goal was to make your own world; form your own reality?" asked Schatten.

"Why not? I expanded its potential. I alone saw what it could do in the proper hands."

"So, you reprogrammed the computer?" asked Schatten.

"No," Karamov responded.

"I thought that was the backbone of the whole thing?" asked Schatten.

"No, no, that was only the process that turned thoughts into actions, but the typewriter itself required modification. I reverse-engineered the original design and recreated it. Then, I alone could control the process to integrate the author with the machine and any storylines. They designed it out, I put it back."

"But how did you keep it a secret from the intelligence community? You couldn't fool everyone."

"The same way you always keep secrets—tell partial truths, blatant lies, and then bribe or eliminate those who would stand in the way of progress. One must have the connections and convince the people in power that it simply was not worth the effort to devote the time and expense necessary to perfect the technology.

"By eliminate, you mean kill?"

"Oh, yes, in some cases. I just followed Stalin's example and tactics that the Russian Mafia adopted. It is the Russian way. By the way, they would have taken it from me had they known the extent of the classified data I was privy to from your database that you stupidly furnished so nicely in your stories. Thank you."

"But if you wield the power to create your own world, why destroy this one? Why kill millions of people?" asked Schatten.

"I would find it difficult to explain to a person like you," said Karamov condescendingly.

"Try me," answered Schatten, seething at the pomposity.

"Power, Mr. Schatten, is everything. It's intoxicating once you possess it. The power of life and death is the pinnacle of existence. To create or destroy is the ultimate game. Besides, if I don't like it, I'll undo it and start over, like any great artist."

"I noticed that you responded to my every move, and it seemed instantaneous. I take it you also modified the system in that regard also to meet your requirements?"

"Of course, dear boy. I couldn't wait days or even hours to make things come about. I saw your plot changes immediately. Yes, once I send in a scenario, it is instantaneous. But I also had help. The Americans modified my machine to receive as well as send. This apparently was done during the transfer of the machines to England, and this modification was never documented. I expanded this feature to be able to monitor anything from any machine in real time, not knowing precisely how many other machines existed. But I did monitor your work on your novel, which I found promising by the way. It tickled me when you created the Viking ship and other drivel when you were experimenting. I was amused because I toyed with the device in the same fashion when I first discovered what it could do. So you see that you were really at a distinct disadvantage, my boy. I knew everything."

"What about error messages?"

"Oh, ridiculous, the machine does that automatically now. The process is completely automated, and the computer works out everything. In fact, it tells me what the corrections were before it publishes the story, as it were. That major glitch was one of the first things patched," replied the Russian. "By the way, the last PS error was a false message; the last chess move; a dagger through the heart as midnight arrived. I know it was melodramatic, but I'm a showman. That, I confess, was me simply having a bit of fun. You see, I sent the error messages directly to your device."

Schatten now knew that the Russian was a narcissist at best and totally mad at worst. It was all a morbid game to him, and the man obviously had no compassion for anyone but himself. He had to do something quick. His time was running out fast, and so were his options.

"I have the capability to control all the other machines. I was toying with you to see how you would respond. I'm sorry, that was cruel in hindsight."

"What?" shouted Schatten, seething. "When do you plan for your storyline to begin? What dictates when the story starts?" asked Schatten.

"There is a green button at the bottom of the typewriter next to the evil little black box. It is the "Go" button. It tells the system when to begin the story. You push this button to tell the computer that once accepted, the story will commence on such and such a date at a prescribed time. But if circumstances arise, the timeline can be reset. The green button can also be set to trigger the plot to begin immediately. This can be accomplished remotely like the professor's group did with your various stories. That is why your stories required no one week interval and occurred in short order. The button was set for the next day. The computer accepted your stories immediately and performed all the corrections required."

"I knew none of this," said an angry Schatten, feeling slighted by the professor. But Schatten wasn't done yet.

"Can I look at the typewriter one last time?" begged Schatten.

"Oh, I suppose the condemned man could be given his last request. Turn around slowly," replied Karamov cocking the gun once more.

As he turned and faced the machine, Schatten hit the send and go buttons and grabbed the unit in one coordinated motion. He then sprang from the chair and rolled toward the door. The outraged Russian dropped the flashlight and fired five sporadic shots into the darkened room. Schatten, lying flat on his back, leaped to his feet and ran toward the dimly lit hallway. He ducked just as the Russian saw him, firing his gun again twice. This time, the searing heat of one of the slugs penetrated the wall and through a gas line. The reaction was almost immediate. As Schatten desperately headed for the next room, keeping as low as he could, the Russian ran out into the hallway and took direct aim upon him; he wouldn't miss this time. As the Russian's finger tightened around the trigger, a huge blast enveloped the entire first floor. It knocked Karamov to the floor before he could pull the trigger and allowed his prey to open the door and enter the next room. Schatten immediately locked the door. Karamov, dazed by the force of the exploding gas main, recovered and got to his feet. He followed Schatten and tried to open the door. Fumbling for his key, he grabbed his gun and fired at the lock. Enraged, he began kicking the door until he finally succeeded in opening it. Schatten took refuge behind a chair in the far, left corner of the room. Now, flames shot up the stairwell and soon moved down the hallway like a raging beast. It was fed by the paintings, tapestries, wallpaper, and the wooden walls. The Russian flipped on the light switch and pointed his weapon, hoping to see his enemy. He looked under the small table before realizing that there was only one spot where the man could hide. He fired another shot in the direction of the chair.

"Come out of there, or I'll kill you where you stand," shouted Karamov.

Schatten had no other choice but follow the man's directive. He slowly rose with the typewriter in hand. As the Russian grinned and drew a bead upon him, the flames entered the room, and half the floor collapsed. Karamov screamed as the flames consumed him, and he plunged down into the smoldering inferno. Schatten watched in horror, pressed up against the back wall. Suddenly, the rest of the floor gave way, and he instinctively grabbed the old radiator located just to his left. At the same time, he released the typewriter, which joined its owner in the massive flames below. Swinging from the radiator and holding on for dear life, he surveyed the room and saw a window just above him. The drapes which covered it caught fire, and he tugged at them until they fell. The flames climbed, consuming everything like searing tentacles trying to envelop him. Schatten pulled himself up until he could stand atop the radiator, grabbing the windowsill for support. He then maneuvered, pulling himself onto the window shelf. Releasing the latch, he pulled upward with all his might until the window opened. This caused a rush of air to draw the flames to him, and the right leg of his sweat suit was suddenly on fire. He dowsed the flames as best he could, but he had to get out now. He crouched down and placed his head through the opening to survey whether the fire had spread to the exterior. Assessing that it was safe, he climbed through to the roof but lost his balance. As if the fire was hunting him, it spread and soon everything around him was ablaze. Schatten rolled down until he caught the edge of the gutter. He hung there for a moment before feeling the heat of the flames that were about to consume him. Releasing his grip, he plunged down to the ground. Briefly assuring that all his body parts functioned, he then ran full speed from the house. Suddenly, a massive explosion rocked the structure, and flames shot out from every angle. *Nothing could live through that,* he thought and momentarily considered trying to recover the typewriter before seeing the folly in it. The sounds of sirens could be heard as people began to emerge from the surrounding area. Schatten stole away through the unlocked gate into the night and never looked back. He took a quick inventory of his wounds and happily was none the worse. He then slowly made his way back to town and the safety of his room.

He thought of what the Russian had said when he cited the passage from Lewis Carroll's *Alice Through the Looking-Glass*. This triggered a flashback of his mother reading him the poem "The Walrus and the Carpenter" from that text at bedtime, which contained the entire verse.

"'The time has come,' the Walrus said, 'To talk of many things: Of shoes—and ships—and sealing-wax—Of cabbages—and kings—And why the sea is boiling hot—And whether pigs have wings.'"

It would never hold the same meaning again.

"I beat you at your own game, Karamov," said Schatten with a smirk as he lay triumphantly on the bed.

It was a victory for the entire the world, but somehow, it was hollow. He had taken a life in the process and felt empty and disgusted. Would he have felt worse if he had stabbed or shot the man to death? He hadn't really beaten the man in the time allowed, and Schatten still felt the sting of being outclassed by his counterpart.

"Death by technology," he said, shaking his head.

Regardless, he had done the job.

18

THE SHADOW WARRIOR

THE NEXT MORNING, SCHATTEN CHECKED out and walked to the train station. He purchased his ticket and asked what time the next train for London Gatwick arrived. It was fortunate that it only required him to wait fifteen minutes. Once on board, he stared out at the countryside but really saw nothing as his mind was consumed by his actions of the previous night. The conductor had to tap Schatten on the shoulder twice before he acknowledged him as the man stamped his ticket. He had put everything right but felt as though a part of him had died. Schatten saw that his best course of action would be to collect his things from the beach house and go home, back to what he knew. There, he could reassess his life and go back to his mundane but safe existence.

This whole thing would make a great book, he thought.

But then he reasoned that no one would buy into the plot. He returned to Boston and picked up his car at the airport and drove back to the beach house and packed his belongings. He had momentarily canvassed the exterior to ensure that no government agent was lying in wait for him to return and arrest him for hacking into the top secret database. He was paranoid at first, anticipating that the desk clerk for the beach house would suddenly point at him as he dropped off his key as two men in black suits seized him. But nothing transpired, and the despondent writer then checked out and drove back to Indianapolis.

Any fears began to dissipate as the cottage disappeared in his rearview mirror. During the long drive home, his mind was in a fog. His actions were governed by a biological autopilot as he instinctively headed for his old apartment complex without thinking. Making his way to his old parking spot, he was irked when he discovered that a Ford SUV occupied his usual space. Even though the parking slots were unassigned, everyone accepted a certain unspoken hierarchy of the tenants based upon longevity. True he had been away for a while, but it felt like the individual failed to honor the code. But at least old Mrs. Thompson still had her old Chevy Nova in the lead spot, where it had been for twenty odd years. This was rather therapeutic in a weird way, just knowing that this microcosm of his old universe hadn't changed. He parked his car and removed his bag from the trunk and looked up to see his apartment, left hand raised to shield his eyes from the sun. He felt rather deflated as the pace had been drastically reduced, and he was no longer running on pure adrenaline. It seemed as though the adventure was now officially over, and cold reality would set in as soon as he entered his apartment. He trudged the metal steps to the second floor of the complex and stood for a moment in front of his door as his mind suddenly relived his adventure. Instinctively, he removed the key ring from his right pocket and inserted his key in the lock. It didn't turn. Schatten tried several times, and nothing happened. Exasperated, he made his way to the manager's office. He entered and found a woman at the desk who asked, "May I help you?"

"Yes, it seems my key doesn't work. I tried it a bunch of times, but it won't turn."

"Which apartment?" she asked.

"27B," he responded.

"And your name?"

"Schatten," he said.

"Just one second while I look it up. You did say 27B?" she asked, searching the computer.

"Yes, is there a problem?"

The woman stopped typing. "Could I see some ID, please?"

Revisionist Future

Schatten fumbled for his wallet and took out his driver's license and gave it to the woman.

"I'm sorry, but we show a Ms. Kilgore as the tenant, Mr. Schatten."

"Why, that's impossible, I've lived here for two years. I just got back in town and paid my rent for three months in advance."

"I'm sorry, but we show that the resident has been with us in that apartment for the last five years."

"What? How can that be?" he snapped.

"Sir, let me see if we have you registered for another apartment."

Looking at her computer screen, the manager looked feverishly but found no Schatten listed.

"I'm terribly sorry, but I find no record of any Schatten over the last twenty years. But we have others available if you'd like to rent from us."

"Wait, ask Mrs. Gamby; she knows me," said Schatten.

"Who?" the manager asked.

"Martha Gamby, the owner," he said.

"Sir, I am the owner and have been for twenty-two years. I bought the apartments from

John Hammel. I'm afraid that I don't know Mrs. Gamby."

"Then what about this key?" he said, removing it from his keychain and presenting it to her.

"Hmm," she said. "It does look similar to one of ours, I'll admit, but that is a fairly common type. I'm sorry, I wish I could be more helpful."

She then handed him back his license and smiled politely. He walked out of the office in a daze, scratching his head. Then he decided to go to the bank and deposit the funds that the professor had given him.

He drove around to the first Capitol Savings and parked his car in the lot. He walked up to one of the tables and retrieved a deposit slip. He then filled it out and decided to keep about $400 in case he needed it for clothes and other necessities while locating another apartment. His mind was a blank, and he couldn't even recall what personal belongings he had left in the apartment. Schatten had stuffed everything but the lamps into his suitcase before he departed so that his trips to the laundromat would be kept to a minimum. He did recall that he hadn't purchased anything new for quite some time. Otherwise, he could have demanded his things from the manager. But he would have looked like an idiot if he had come back with, "I can't recall what they were, but they were worth a lot."

He made his way to the teller and handed her his deposit slip.

A puzzled look then gripped her face as she studied the computer screen.

"I'm sorry, but I can't find you in our system. Are you sure you're in the right bank?" she said.

"What?" said Schatten. "I've been doing business here for ten years; it must be in there."

"You can talk to the manager if you'd like," she said.

"Yes, that would be fine," he responded, perplexed.

She picked up a phone and then talked to someone.

"He'll be right with you, sir," she said politely.

In a few minutes, a man in a blue coat and tie greeted him.

"What seems to be the issue?" he asked the teller.

"This gentleman would like to make a deposit, but nothing shows up in the system," she said.

"Let's see. Excuse me just a minute," he said, preparing to search through the computer.

"Your name please?" he asked.

"Schatten."

"No, I am sorry but that name isn't here. But we'd be pleased to open an account for you."

"Ah, no, no thanks, just the same," he said.

He walked out, angry and confused. Then he decided to visit the office of his publicist. He drove to the location downtown and parked a block away since there was limited space in front of the facility. He went into the building and scanned the directory.

"Hellen Hunt, Hellen Hunt," he said as he perused all the listings. "Come on," he said angrily, as he failed to find her name anywhere.

Then he used his cell phone and dialed her number. It rang several times before the automatic voice response said, "We're sorry, that number has been disconnected or is no longer in service."

He then looked through his glove compartment and found his registration. It contained his old address except the apartment number was wrong. It said 2E not 2B. He went over to the apartment building once more and ran up the steps.

There was no apartment 2E. Now he was in a panic. He quickly removed his wallet and took out his driver's license and read the data. There was the same address with apartment 2E. How could that be? Why hadn't he noticed this previously?

In desperation, he fumbled for Chelston's number. Finding it, he couldn't push the buttons fast enough. The phone rang for what seemed an hour before a voice answered, "Hello."

"Hello, hello, Professor Chelston, is that you?" he said in desperation.

"Yes, it is, who am I speaking with?"

"It's Michael, Michael Schatten."

"Well, Michael, nice to hear from you. Is anything wrong?"

"Yes, everything is wrong. I really need to see you; will you be in town tomorrow?"

"Yes, I'll be home in the afternoon, any time after one."

"Great, I'll see you then."

Schatten looked at his gas gauge and went to the nearest service station. Placing his credit card in the pump, he took a deep sigh of relief when the transaction went through and the gas began to flow.

At least something works, he thought.

Still in a panic, he began to be more objective and think through all the possibilities as to who was responsible for his current position. But as he filled his tank, he suddenly remembered the professor's warning when he had stayed too long in the secret database.

They must have found me, he thought.

Schatten was referring to the government agents who were monitoring the classified site. He had recalled the stories from TV shows and internet conspiracy sites that told of such things. They described how people's lives had been ruined and discredited by the men in black; those faceless, nameless individuals who toiled for secret federal organizations and seemingly knew everything about everyone. They possessed the power to erase college transcripts, birth certificates, and employment histories. These shadowy figures also had the ability to make people and bank accounts disappear. In retrospect, he thought that using his credit card might have been a bad idea since they could track his whereabouts through his purchases. Chelston could confirm this for he would know, he had to know; the professor was his only hope.

His paranoia induced him to drive through the night until he reached the little New England town where the good professor resided. Schatten parked as close as he could and raced to Chelston's home. Huffing and puffing, he sprinted to the door and rang the bell. When Chelston appeared, Schatten felt as though he had gotten a reprieve from the insanity of the past hours.

"You look positively pale, dear boy. Do come in," said the professor.

"Professor, I don't know where else to turn," said Schatten.

"Well come in and have some tea and a sandwich, and let's get to the bottom of all that's troubling you, shall we?" he said reassuringly, placing his hand on Schatten's shoulder. "Have a seat in the study, and I'll fix you something. I think I'm down to pepper cheese, but I have some excellent French bread."

"That will do fine," responded Schatten.

Schatten paced while his host made the tea and a sandwich and started to hyperventilate. In a few minutes, the professor returned and handed Schatten the sandwich and placed the tea on the coffee table in front of him.

"Please sit down, and don't look so flustered," said Chelston. "What's troubling you, son. I would have thought that you would have been elated."

"Elated? Elated over what?" asked Schatten, grabbing the sandwich and taking a large bite.

He hadn't eaten in some time and didn't realize the extent of his hunger. Then Chelston laid a copy of the *Boston Globe* newspaper in front of him, folded to page four. The headline read, "Renowned Russian author killed in house fire."

"I assume that this is your handiwork? I think congratulations are in order. Well done, Michael. The country, no, the world owes you a great debt."

"Speaking of debt, I believe you owe me five hundred grand. It will help ease the pain. It hardly feels like a ringing victory," said Schatten despondently. "Taking a life is not something you just blot out of your memory."

"Yes, I can see that, but it wasn't like you took a life indiscriminately. You may have very well saved humanity. We decorate our war heroes and those who protect us from evil men, but that doesn't mean they don't have a conscience too and that they don't feel the same as you. It is perfectly natural to feel guilt and remorse even though the cause was just. But don't be too hard on yourself, you did what the US military and intelligence community failed to do. But if I may ask, how did you do it?"

Schatten confided that he had used the Russian's own modifications of the typewriter against him. Before Karamov had appeared, Schatten suddenly got the idea to write the man's destruction with Karamov's own machine once he found it.

Schatten put down his food and drank some tea to wash it down.

Then Chelston handed him a slip of paper. "Here is the account number and your pass code for the Swiss account."

"But how did you know the layout of his house, which room it would be in, and that his house was a two-story dwelling?"

"I didn't know what room precisely, so I just searched for it. I looked up the floor plan on the internet before I left the beach house when I was killing time awaiting his responses."

"But the fire, how did you escape, and what of his typewriter?" asked Chelston, intently listening to ever word.

"I didn't know if the SAM computer had approved my submittal in Boston. When I found the typewriter, I thought of grabbing it and running, but I was suddenly overcome by the urge to compose Karamov's demise. I would use the same instrument he used to bring about the destruction of the world, as the weapon to defeat him. I wrote a quick story and was ready to send it when he caught me unawares and held a gun to my head. I bought just enough time to press the send button when he let his guard down for a split second.

"That's quite a tale, young man, but why didn't you contact me after it all happened?"

"I guess I wanted to put everything behind me and just go home," lamented Schatten. "But you can't go home again."

The professor looked rather nervous as he asked, "Other than quoting Mr. Wolfe, what do you mean, dear boy?"

"You know, it's funny, but Karamov called me "dear boy" as well. Professor, everything in my life is coming apart like a bad dream," Schatten said.

"So, I sense that there is something more than taking the man's life troubling you. Tell me everything," said Chelston.

"I went home, but I have no apartment anymore, I have no bank account, I have no . . ."

Then Schatten took out his driver's license and handed it to Chelston. "How do you explain that?" Schatten asked. "It's the wrong apartment. It doesn't exist. It's like that on any ID I have with an address. It's the government, isn't it? I stayed too long in the database, and they tracked me down, didn't they? By the way, how did you know I was in the classified database when you called?"

"We monitor anyone that enters and keep track of their time inside. We can't afford to allow anyone to know that we have access. It's an electronic display on our computers that monitors anyone with the capability to enter, like you, Michael. To answer your other question, no, my boy, you are not being followed, I can assure you," Chelston responded, with a wry smile.

Chelston studied the license carefully and then rose from his chair, placing his right hand over his mouth.

He walked over to the other side of the room and then walked back before handing the laminated card to Schatten.

"Let me tell you a story. But first, Michael, let me say that everyone, the world in general, owes you a debt more than we ever can repay. Those of us who knew you will remember that you were unique, an icon as it were. I knew this time might come, but I never really prepared for it," he said, fumbling to choose his words carefully.

Schatten was confused.

"What's going on, Professor. Tell me straight. You owe me that much."

The professor paused and looked at Schatten briefly.

With head down, he again walked to the other side of the room, stroking the hair at the base of his neck before turning to say, "Yes, Michael, I'm afraid I do."

"Please go on," said Schatten, almost shaking with anticipation.

The professor sighed, finding it difficult to select the right words.

"Michael, when we constructed the system of which the typewriters were a part, we tried to envision how the whole thing would function. We tried to imagine what it would be like creating actual living, breathing entities. It was almost like playing God. We created many types of individuals from accountants to scientists. We dubbed them shadow warriors, or simply shadows. We thought that we had it all figured out to the nth degree, when one of the people we used as the donor became very ill and almost died."

"Donor?" asked Schatten.

"Forgive me. It's the term we employed for the individual who would serve as the source for the extraction of the energy required to create our duplicate artificial person; the doppelgänger. Recall that the creation of an artificial person was based upon Einstein's theory that it was possible to fashion a mirror image of an actual living, breathing human. We couldn't merely fabricate a character out of thin air. The energy had to be drawn from a real person."

"Okay, I'm with you. We talked of this before. Go on," said Schatten consuming his sandwich.

"When the first person inside the group who volunteered to be the donor collapsed, we knew it was time to reassess our procedures. It was as if the very life had been drawn out of him, for want of a better description."

"Did this person make a full recovery?" asked Schatten.

"Yes, but only under intensive care for weeks. It wasn't something that any of us wanted to see again, I assure you. So we developed safety procedures, 'protocols,' as we called them to prevent a repetition of such circumstances. We limited the longevity of our characters to less than two weeks by building the time into the plot," explained Chelston.

"What actually becomes of the characters after the time expires?" This was a question that Schatten had asked himself as he created his artificial characters from his novel.

"They simply fade to black," said Chelston.

"So they simply fade away, into nothing? Is that what you're saying?"

"Precisely," responded Chelston.

"How do you know that these characters of yours don't take kindly to their termination? How do you know what they feel, especially in those last desperate minutes before they 'fade to black' as you say?"

"We don't know that at all, Michael. None of them had ever been around to tell us," he replied. "But there would be telltale signs."

"Like what?" asked Schatten.

"They would simply begin to fade from history. Their identity would start to erode, their memories would begin to fade, and all traces of who they were, like bank accounts, places of residence, and driver's license dates would begin to simply fade away," he said softly.

"Why didn't you send one of them to do your dirty work and eliminate Karamov?" asked Schatten.

"We did," replied Chelston, looking at Schatten like a father telling his son that he was diagnosed with some incurable disease. "We sent you."

Schatten froze. He had heard what the man said, but it didn't quite register. He didn't want it to register. His lips moved as he tried to respond, but his voice failed him. He was overcome with emotion unlike he had ever experienced.

"Do you know the origin of your name?" asked Chelston. "It's German for shadow."

Chelston was in a very awkward position now, for he was totally unprepared of what to do next.

It was a situation that he had never really contemplated even though it was a main element in the unscripted experimental process of communicating with this doppelgänger.

"You mean I'm, I'm . . . ?" said Schatten in a desperate tone.

"Michael, I'm merely stating fact. You are a shadow warrior. The best that's ever been created. You are the first free-thinking entity who was allowed to write your own script. You found a way to get the job done against all odds."

"You're saying I'm experiencing the stages of a character on his way to oblivion? I'm just supposed to go quietly into the night?"

"Michael, calm down, please," said Chelston in a consoling tone.

Schatten rose from his chair and began pacing furiously, shaking his head.

"Michael, please sit down."

"Sit down? Will that make this all go away? Wait, wait, you said that your characters wouldn't have any memories," said Schatten in a raised tone, pointing at the professor with his right index finger. "Well, I have all of mine. I can remember my mom and my dad and where I grew up."

"Okay, where are your parents now?" asked Chelston.

"They're in, they're in . . . I can't remember," responded Schatten.

"What were their names?" asked Chelston.

"Uh, Al and Megon," he replied sharply.

"Those are the names of the parents of Daniel Belamy from Heller, Wisconsin," replied Chelston.

"Well, who is Daniel whatever, and why should I care?"

"He is your donor; the person from whom you draw all your memories, and you are his doppelgänger, his duplicate. If you stay much longer, he will not survive. Surely you wouldn't want that? He has a wife and two children."

Schatten suddenly felt trapped and had trouble breathing, as if a noose had been tied around his neck. His logic was fading fast, and his mind failed to fully grasp or accept everything that had been thrown at him. Then anger overcame him.

Schatten reacted defensively in the only way left open to him; he simply began to reject Chelston's contentions.

"Michael, if it's any consolation, you were programmed to kill Karamov by any means necessary. You were compelled to carry it out. Countering Karamov's plot was a no-win scenario; an exercise in initiative. So you don't have to shoulder that blame for his death. We wrote that into your storyline."

"I suppose you wrote how I found the typewriter in the first place?"

"Yes, it was all part of the basic plot," responded Chelston.

"That's absurd, all of this is absurd. I've heard enough. I've done everything that you asked of me, and all I get are lies and ridiculous assertions. I came here for your help and some reasonable explanation for everything that's coming down on me. If you think that I'm gonna listen to any more of this, you are sadly mistaken. I'm outta here," said Schatten, bolting for the front door.

Chelston went after him, but the man sprinted away, and there was no hope he'd return.

EPILOGUE
I AM SAM

A WEEK PASSED AS PROFESSOR CHELSTON sat in his study on a quiet Sunday afternoon. As he began to drift off while reading *The Old Man and the Sea*, his solitude was broken rather dramatically by a knock at the door. The professor slowly rose from his chair and put down his book. He then slowly strode down the hallway to the front door and opened it reticently, as though seeing the foreshadowing of some calamity. As he opened the door and his eyes focused upon the interloper to his peaceful afternoon, he was stunned to see Carl Edlin, who seemed rather upset. Edlin was one of the chief physicists who had been a part of the secret program that had developed the shadow warriors. He was the person who posed as the shopkeeper and sold Schatten his typewriter. Edlin was an integral part of writing the storylines and composing the characters for the various plots that altered history.

He was employed by the US intelligence agency which still sponsored and created the covert operations that these two men had started so long ago.

"Carl, what brings you here?" asked the professor.

Edlin looked behind him as though he was being followed, then abruptly entered the house without even the slightest hint of an invitation.

"Everet! Everet, we have a problem! At least a potential one—at least, I think we have a potential issue," blurted out Edlin, visibly shaken.

"Carl, let me make some tea. You'll feel better. Please have a seat in the study."

"I don't need any tea, just answers," replied Edlin.

"Alright," said Chelston, stopping in his tracks.

He ushered his guest into the study and put his hand on his shoulder.

"Now what's this all about, what has you in such a state? Have a seat."

Edlin took a piece of paper from his pocket and handed it to Chelston.

Chelston scanned the text and read it through twice, eyebrows raised. The computer printer readout was succinct. "Michael Anniston Schatten will be allowed to live on and experience and find the meaning of all the facets of life. He will be unencumbered and allowed free rein of all his activities. He will live on as he so chooses to be whatever and whoever he desires."

There was nothing else.

"Where did you get this?" he asked his guest.

"From the institute. They were running a routine security diagnostic on the mainframe when they found this."

"Someone attempted to get this through the system?" asked Chelston.

"No. Someone already got that through the system. It's been approved," replied Edlin.

"That's impossible! How could . . . ?"

Both men looked at each other, and Chelston now understood his guest's concern.

"You mean he found a way into the computer without anyone monitoring his activities and got around all the safeguards?" asked Chelston, still fixated on the text.

"Apparently, yes. He wrote his own ticket. He found a way to interface with it directly. We don't know the extent of his submissions, only what you see. He wanted us to find this," added Edlin.

"It's a joke, Carl. Someone is having a good laugh at your expense. I had our Mr. Schatten taken into custody and had the computer brought directly here for safekeeping. It's in my upstairs safe. I'll show you," said Chelston, chuckling and confident. "After all, I did have a conversation with him."

"You what? That wasn't in the script; he really did that on his own?"

"Come now, Carl, have a little faith. You know that it was a major part of the experiment, to see if the character could freelance. Well he did, and better than any of us envisioned. He came up with his own plot to eliminate Karamov. He felt deep remorse and actually went home. Unfortunately, things weren't what he remembered, and he came here for answers."

"But there was no home. How could he return to a place that never existed, except in his mind?" asked Edlin.

"Well his memories were there, which resulted in some traumatic events, such as having the wrong apartment number on his driver's license, no apartment, or bank account. Imagine how that would scare you, Carl?"

"So you actually talked to him, in a meaningful way? You actually had a spontaneous interaction with the character? What did you tell him?" asked Edlin in disbelief.

"I told him the truth about who he was and how he should feel proud of his accomplishments," replied Chelston.

"And what was his response?"

"He accused me of lying and bolted out the door. There was no reasoning with him. He was totally irrational," said Chelston in a despondent tone. "After that, I decided to call the intelligence types and have him picked up and taken to a safe place, just in case. You should have seen the anger in his eyes."

"So he must have written this before you arrested him?" said Edlin.

"Carl, we didn't arrest him, he was merely moved to a secure location where he lived out his final hours, under observation. I even have the video of him and signed affidavits to attest that fact from the people assigned to be with him up to the last moments," said a confident Chelston.

"And when were you planning to share all this?" asked Edlin, perturbed.

"When I handed in the full report. Karamov was gone and threat was ended, I saw no need to rush," responded Chelston coldly.

"Now I'd really like to see the typewriter. It would make me feel a lot better," said Edlin.

They walked upstairs to a locked room with a steel door. Chelston pressed a series of buttons on an electronic combination lock and opened the door. He switched on the light and went to a picture hanging at the back of the small room. He removed it to expose a wall safe, and he dialed in a combination.

Then he pulled a handle and opened the two-foot, square door.

"Here we are, Carl, my friend. See for yourself," said Chelston, stepping out of the way.

Peering inside, his associate exclaimed, "Everet, there's nothing here!"

"Don't be ridiculous, I placed it in there myself," snapped Chelston condescendingly.

To his embarrassment, he saw that Edlin was absolutely correct; the safe was empty.

"Who else has the combination to this?" asked Edlin.

"No one," responded Chelston in amazement. "But we had him in custody and the device as well, and he had no access to it," said a bewildered Chelston.

"How long a period elapsed from the time he left to the time when the agents took him into custody?" asked Edlin.

"Oh, it couldn't have been that long; a day perhaps. Why do you ask?" asked Chelston.

"Let me check on something. Can I use your phone?" asked Edlin.

Edlin then placed a call and then promptly hung up.

"What was that about?" asked Chelston.

"We'll see in few minutes. I'm having something checked out. It might be nothing, but then again . . ."

In a few minutes, the phone rang, and Chelston answered it.

"It's for you," he said, handing it to Edlin.

Edlin listened intently and jotted down a few words on a notepad that Chelston kept by his phone. Then he responded, "Thank you very much. Could you fax me the entire transcript?" Then he put his hand over the phone and asked Chelston, "Do you have a fax machine here?"

"Yes," replied Chelston and wrote down the number for Edlin, who promptly passed it over to the person at the other end. In a few minutes, the fax machine in the corner of the room next to the computer printed out several pages of text.

"Here is the entire interaction of Mr. Schatten with the main computer," said Edlin, picking up the transmission.

"Well it seems that Mr. Schatten was very busy from the time he left here, judging from the date and times of these transmissions. He went back to Salisbury England, recovered the typewriter, and returned," commented Edlin, perusing the three pages of text.

"Here, read this," he said as Chelston snatched the full readout.

Chelston froze in his tracks. The text he scanned was the chronology of Schatten's entries into the computer, hours before their agents apprehended the person who they thought was Schatten. The text read, "Entity number two and machine two are to be created and appear at coordinates FB56/UG70."

Instead, it was clear that their own creation had become a creator in his own right as the reference to entity two and machine two described.

"Apparently, he's developed some sort of a code that cannot be broken at this time. But some of the transmissions were in plain English, as though he's taunting us," said Edlin solemnly, exhaling.

"He made a surrogate?" asked Chelston.

"Apparently," offered Edlin, scarcely able to comprehend the enormity and horrifying significance of this revelation.

"It seems that we had a temporary copy of Mr. Schatten and his typewriter. He also apparently retrieved Karamov's typewriter from the ashes in Salisbury. The letter and number combinations are for the exact location where it would be found. The text says, "The Karamov machine, unharmed, will be found by Schatten at the southwest corner of the house under stone debris, coordinates YN54/UG 92."

"But he told me that it had been destroyed," said Chelston.

"Well if you read on, you will see that he resurrected it himself. Then he wrote his own ticket home, out of the country, and through customs. He now is in possession of not only his device but Karamov's. Only Mr. Schatten now knows the extent of Karamov's modifications," lamented Edlin.

"We have a man's life to think about here also," said Chelston. "The real person who we used to create the doppelgänger will die if Schatten continues. We have to stop him, Carl!"

Edlin just smirked.

"We're talking about a life, Carl, I hardly think that is a joking matter."

"Apparently, he was able to work around that one as well. He's drawing from various people at various times to serve his purpose," replied Edlin. "He circumvented the system."

"How could you know that?" asked Chelston.

"Because the man who served as his source, who he mirrored, is quite well it seems. Remember how we instituted the system to monitor how much energy was being drawn from any one person when we created the doppelgängers?" asked Edlin.

"Of course; the safety net, the safeguard system to prevent anyone from having the life inadvertently, totally drained out of them," recalled Chelston.

"Well, it is showing nothing being drawn from the original donor, and it is unclear as to which individual he's drawing from now, since its constantly changing," finished Edlin.

"If that's the case, who are we dealing with now; Michael Schatten or someone else?" asked Chelston.

"Only God and Michael Schatten know the answer to that riddle," said Edlin.

Now on a hill overlooking the Atlantic Ocean, the entity created as Michael Schatten, glanced into the night sky and composed a short letter to his surrogate father, Everet Chelston. He thanked him for everything he had done but would never forgive him for putting him in the position to take a human life. He also added that, as of this writing, Michael Schatten would no longer exist. As to whom he would become, Schatten wrote, "If you desire to know just who I am, read Dr. Seuss's *Green Eggs and Ham*."

Chelston received the letter a few days later and called Edlin over to read the contents. Coldly and calmly, Chelston purged the emotion from his mind. He now looked upon all that transpired with Schatten as he would a virus that had mutated. When Edlin arrived, Chelston gave him the letter, and it stunned the man.

Edlin could only utter, "Green Eggs and Ham?"

Chelston walked over to one of the bookshelves in his study. He removed a thin orange book and handed it to Edlin. "I keep this for my grandson. It's his favorite. Read the first page."

"I am Sam? Sam I am?" asked Edlin with a blank stare.

"Don't you see?" Chelston said.

"See what?"

"Schatten, or whatever his name is now, is SAM—the computer!" shouted Chelston. "He's made himself another part of the system that can't be switched off."

Schatten was privy to everything inside the mighty SAM computer. He could now be who he wished, whenever he wished, without impacting anyone. Thanks to Karamov's modifications, he was able to write scenarios and have them instantly turned into reality. But even of more significance was the fact that his mind meshed with that of SAM. His capabilities were endless, and he became a new life-form. It gave new meaning to the term Artificial Intelligence.

Schatten had not only been able to interface with the system but done so in ways beyond everyone's comprehension.

Just to make his point that he was an incremental part of the system, he wrote, "If you ever need to contact me just type in *Incursion of Shadows*." This was the top secret code from their superiors at the highest level that signified for them to write a mission for the shadow warriors. It was only known to four individuals, and one was the president. They were horrified, and the silence lasted for several minutes.

"Notice how he ends the letter," said Chelston, trying to fathom the magnitude of it all.

Edlin read everything and paused at the bottom of the page.

The letter finished with, "I have been engaged in countless hours of study and introspection, and I found the phrase that best describes me: Cogito, ergo sum."

"We both know the translation," said Chelston.

"Yes, he's quoting Descartes," replied Edlin, shaken with a wry smile. "I think therefore I am."

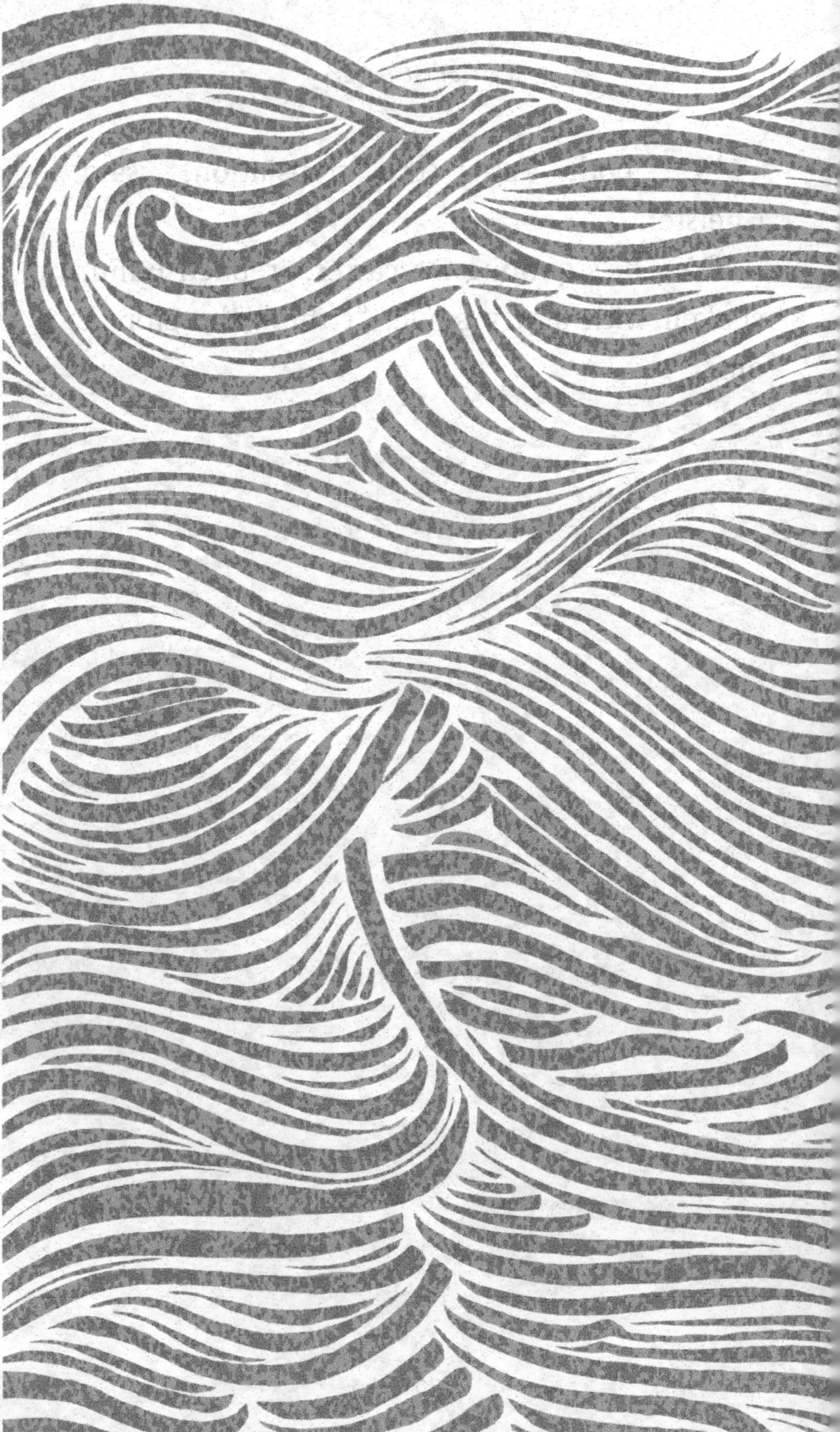

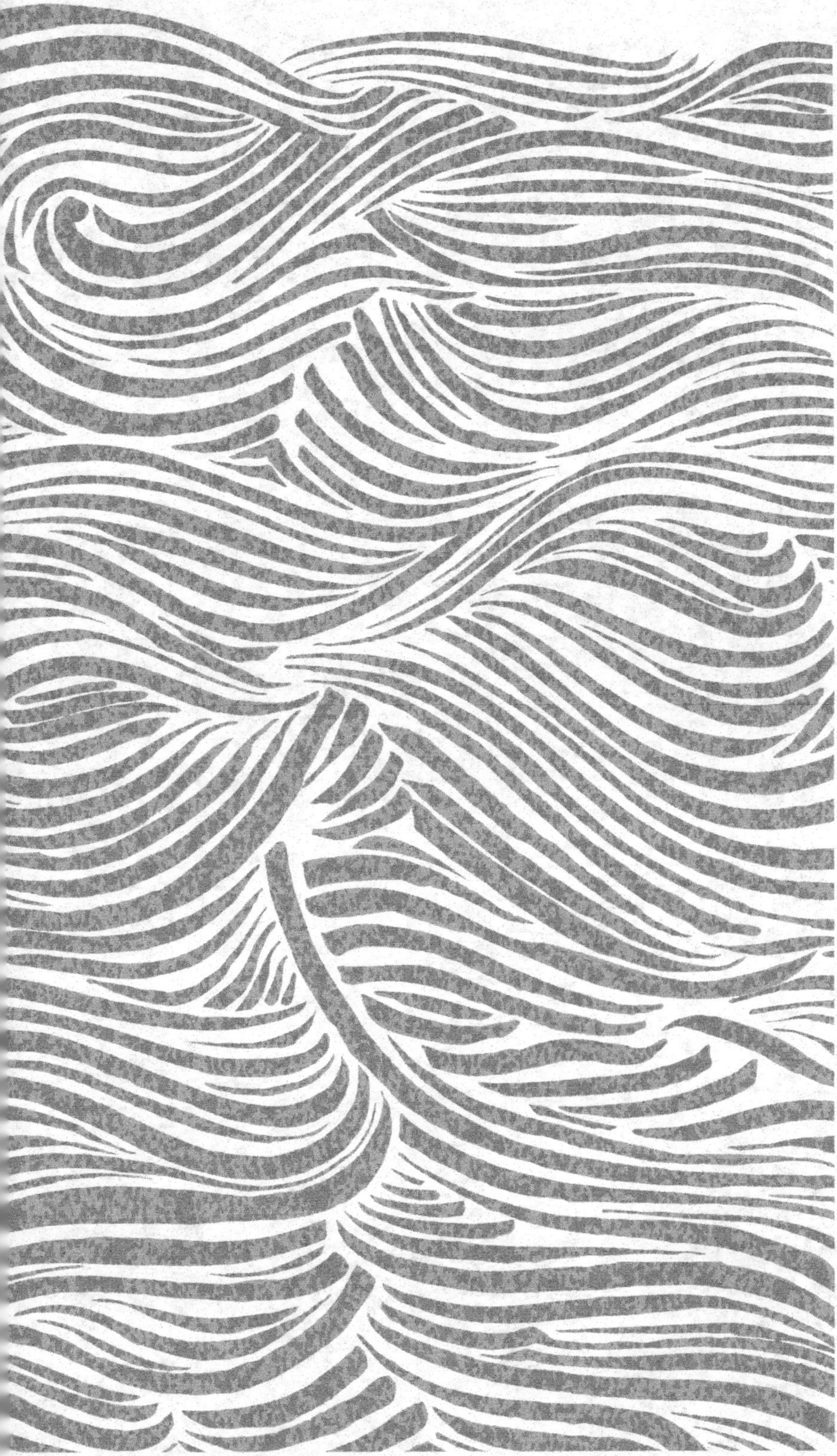

ACKNOWLEDGMENTS

Thanks so much to my sister for reading my work and never pulling punches in her commentary.

ABOUT THE AUTHOR

Lee Bumbicka is the child of a US Army officer and an English war bride. He started writing when he was a teenager but became a serious author in 1997. He is an Aerospace engineer, with a degree from the University of Missouri, Rolla. He is married, has two children, and a sister who also writes.

When he is not writing, Lee builds (and collects) vintage model kits, and watches sports.

He has also been seen playing golf and tennis. On his long walks, he contemplates new stories to tell. His goal is to make the reader think, *I didn't see that coming.*

If you enjoyed Lee Bumbicka's
Revisionist Future,
you'll also enjoy
A Grave Too Many by William Norris.

While long on the run from Afrikaner nationalists, commercial pilot John Kruger discovers that the body of his hero WWI flying ace Andrew Beauchamp-Proctor was buried in two graves 6,000 miles apart. One pilot's secret could be another's catastrophe.

CHAPTER ONE

THE SHADOW OF THE ANCIENT biplane danced and fluttered over Salisbury Plain. Etched sharp by the bright May sunshine, the SE5a ran on toward the village, growing larger as it descended in a graceful turn toward the grass landing strip. The young pilot scanned the ground from the open cockpit. He watched the racing shadow flick across thatched roofs and rambling gardens, touching the village graveyard with a passing shroud and moving swiftly on. On a bench beside the tombstones, he could see, quite clearly, the upturned face of a tiny seated figure. The figure waved. Beneath his goggles, the pilot grinned and raised a gloved hand to return the salute before concentrating once more on his approach and landing. It would not do to bend it; this was the only one left. The very last genuine SE5a in the whole damn world, outside of a museum.

 He lined up the blunt engine cowling with the runway markers and moved the throttle quadrant until the roar of the Hispano-Suiza engine subsided to a gentle burble. The nose of the SE5a sank into a long, gliding approach and the ground rose up to meet it. Now, a steady pull on the cord-bound ring of the joystick, and the rate of descent eased. He shifted his gaze to the side as the long cowling rose to cut his forward vision, and watched the blades of grass racing by beneath the trailing edges of the lower wings. The noise of the wind in the wires died away, the stick was back in his belly, and he felt a small jar through the airframe as the tail skid touched fractionally before the main wheels. There were no brakes. The SE5a bumped along gently for fifty yards and rolled to a halt. He gave it a small burst of throttle, turned, and taxied slowly toward the hangar.

"She's fine," he told the waiting mechanic. "Just fine." He gave the side of the cockpit an affectionate pat and walked away slowly with real regret. They did not make them like that anymore, and it was a pity. That was the end of true flying for a month, until they let him take the old warplane up again on the next public-display day. Tomorrow he would be back in the draftless efficiency of a Boeing 747, hauling tourists and businessmen on the long flight to New York. It was a living, but that was all. The pilot left his helmet on, the goggles pushed up on his forehead, as he wandered through the ice-cream-licking crowds to the 1946 MG sports car that was his second love. Truth to tell, he rather enjoyed the Red Baron image. He caught the admiring glances of several attractive girls and flicked the silk scarf back around his neck.

Then, clambering into the vestigial cockpit of the MG, he nudged it into life and set off down the hill. There was one more thing he wanted to do before he left Upavon that day.

The old man had been dreaming. It was a familiar dream, and he savored it with a smile as he dozed on the green bench beside the upright sentinels of the grave markers. The graves around him were mostly of airmen—relics of the days long ago when Upavon had been an operational airfield in two world wars. Perhaps, he often thought, that was the reason the dream came most vividly when he sat on this bench.

He had not slept long—only closing his eyes when the SE5a sank behind the trees on the ridge across the valley—but the dream had carried him back more than sixty years, to the days of his youth and a muddy field close to the Allied lines on the western front.

It was 1917, a fine September morning, and the noise of the guns in the distance was almost drowned out by birdsong. Outside the makeshift hangars in a field on the outskirts of Flez, a line of SE5a's had just returned from dawn patrol. Mechanics fussed around them as a truck deposited the trio of replacement pilots outside the tent that served as squadron headquarters.

The war was at its height and not going well. The French army had mutinied, and in the mud and devastation of the Ypres Salient, more than a half million men were dying in the bitter struggle for a place called Passchendaele.

None of it seemed to matter as he stood there in his high-buttoned tunic with shining Royal Flying Corps wings on the left breast. Seven months before, he had been an engineering student at Cape Town University who had never even seen an airplane. Now he was an operational fighter pilot.

"Hey, Shorty!" The reverie within a dream was interrupted. A young man in a leather flying jacket was calling to him from the flight line. "Do you think you can fly one of these things? I reckon you won't see out of the cockpit."

The newcomer rummaged in the top of his kit bag and produced a pair of leather-covered cushions, brandishing them at the other pilot. "No problem," he shouted back. Jibes about his lack of height had once upset him, but now he had ceased to care. If God had meant him to grow taller than five foot two, God would doubtless have done something about it. God had made him a fighter pilot. That was what mattered.

The dream skipped in time, and now he was in the air, screaming down out of the sun at full throttle toward the unsuspecting Rumpler two-seater that was climbing for height far below him. Too late, the enemy pilot realized his danger and began to turn away. But the twin Vickers machine guns were cocked and ready, and he saw the German observer crumple as he poured the first burst into the rear cockpit.

A wild cavorting in the sky, two more bursts, and the Rumpler was falling like a bird with a broken wing. He saw it crash into a field beside the silver thread of the river Somme and burst into flames.

The old man stirred awake. His cheeks were wet for the thought of the men he had killed. So many men. Fifty-four victories, they said, but those were only the kills that could be confirmed. And all in those thirteen savage months before the Armistice brought the madness to a close. So many men. So many widows.

He opened his eyes slowly, feeling cheated. The dream had ended before its usual climax: the scene he cherished most, where he stood in the long room at Buckingham Palace, and the bearded, long-dead king pinned the medals on his chest. The Victoria Cross, the Distinguished Service Order, the Military Cross and the Distinguished Flying Cross. More medals than any South African had ever won. Medals to mark his achievement as the fifth-ranking ace in the whole of the Allied air force. Medals he had not seen for years, tucked away in a secret drawer in the back of his writing bureau.

The voice that woke him had a familiar inflection. It startled him.

"Sir, forgive me, but I've been wanting to meet you for months."

The voice was out of his boyhood—the flat nasal drawl of the highveld. But its owner . . . Dear God, thought the old man, I must have died in my sleep, or else I am dreaming still. The flying helmet, the goggles, the silk scarf and leather jacket . . . it's Harry van der Merwe, my old wingman from Eighty-Four Squadron.

But van der Merwe was dead, long dead. He had flown out to meet Baron Manfred von Richthofen's circus in the cold light of dawn and had never returned. The old man closed his eyes again and opened them slowly. The apparition was still there.

He struggled stiffly to his feet. Age had diminished him further, and he stood no taller than the pilot's chest.

"Who . . . who are you?" There was no sign of a South African accent in his own voice. That had long since gone.

"Sir, my name is John Kruger. I'm the pilot of that SE5a you waved to a short time ago. I've seen you here, on the same spot, every time I fly over. You always wave, and I always wave back. I thought it was time we got acquainted.

I was just curious, I guess," he added lamely. A wary look, almost hostile, had come into the old man's eyes.

"You're not English," the old man challenged.

"No, sir. As a matter of fact I come from South Africa."

"Go away," the old man said. "Leave me alone. I'm English, damn you. This is my country. We don't want any bloody Boers over here. Be off with you." He raised his stick. The pilot stepped back quickly.

"But sir, I only thought, because you seemed so interested in the plane—"

"Young man, I have no interest in aeroplanes, and I have never waved to one in my life. I come here sometimes for peace and quiet. That is all." He gestured toward the gravestones beside the graveled path. "I want to be left in peace with my friends."

Kruger's eyes followed the movement, taking in the neat rows of uniform headstones and the well-kept lawn. Suddenly he froze. "That's odd," he said. "This grave over here. I've never been to this cemetery, but I could swear that

I've seen that name before." He shook his head in puzzlement and moved closer to one stone standing in the center of a row of three. The old man remained perfectly still, save for the pulse of a swollen vein beating in his temple.

Kruger read the headstone aloud. "Flight Lieutenant Andrew Weatherby Beauchamp-Proctor VC, DSO, MC, DFC. Killed at Upavon, June 21, 1921." Beneath the inscription was a replica of the Victoria Cross, and the inscription "For Valour."

He straightened up, his voice excited. "But I know this guy. At least, I know of him. He was the local hero back in my hometown, Mafeking. When we were at school we all learned about Andrew Proctor and the way he won the VC. Why, he used to fly SE5a's, too. Perhaps that's why I got mixed up in this business. But . . . ." Kruger paused, his brow furrowed. "He can't be buried here. I mean, he's buried back home in Mafeking. I know he is. I've seen the grave. I . . . I don't understand."

He turned to look at the old man, but found he was talking to himself. Through the gates of the cemetery, fifty yards away, the small black figure of the man was hurrying away down the hill, coat flapping, as though the devil himself were in pursuit.

Kruger stood by the grave of Andrew Beauchamp-Proctor for several minutes, deep in thought. "Queer," he murmured. "Very queer. Whoever heard of a man being buried in two places at once?"

He walked slowly back to his car and drove away along the winding Wiltshire lanes.

CamCat Books

VISIT US ONLINE FOR
MORE BOOKS TO LIVE IN:
CAMCATBOOKS.COM

FOLLOW US

CamCatBooks   @CamCatBooks   @CamCat_Books